AVERY'S WAY

F. L. Goltz

MAY: 1999

Tom:
It truly was a
pleasure seeing you and
your wife over the Mother's day
weekend. I hope all is going well
with you and your family. I also
hope you enjoy "Avery's way" 1st.
Book in the Avery Proffrock
Series.

Your Friend
F. L. Goltz

VANTAGE PRESS
New York

AVERY'S WAY

To my wife, Karen,
who made it possible

Prologue

Avery Profrock was enjoying a successful career writing suspense novels based on experiences from his secret past. The future looked good.

When tragedy strikes and he learns that the explosion, and fire, that killed his wife and niece was not an accident, he sets out to find the people responsible. His search leads him into partnership with a displaced Witness Protection Program director who knows Avery's secret past. Danger awaits them, danger because the people they are going after are powerful and getting more powerful each day. . . .

Avery must kill again!

AVERY'S WAY

1

Dredging and blasting along the lake shoreline had been going on since early March after the winter ice cleared out. The lake was normally teeming with sport fishermen throughout the spring and summer; however, the ongoing bridge construction spooked the fish, and anglers opted for other lakes in the area. The construction created financial hardships for many of the local businesses, who depended on the money generated by the sportsmen to see them through until the skiing season that began in mid-November.

Influential residents helped by putting pressure on the construction company to get the blasting done that year. Everyone wanted interruptions to the local economy and world-famous musical institute to end as soon as possible. County ordinances were amended temporarily so the construction company could conduct blasting into the evening hours and weekends. These changes would help bring this phase of the operation to a quick end with the least amount of inconvenience.

Locals became accustomed to the sporadic thumps and bangs of blasting, including one of the lake's noted residents, Avery Profrock, and his brother, Carl. Out on the lake that evening nothing seemed amiss in Avery's twenty-six-foot runabout cruiser. He and Carl were preparing for a night of stargazing through the new telescope Avery's publishing agent had given him for just such an occasion. Blasting was being done on this night also, but something was nagging at Avery and he couldn't quite put his finger on what was wrong. It was well past dark when he realized that one of the blasts had not been preceded by the complimentary three short toots from an airhorn introducing the impending intrusion into everyone's lives. Avery didn't recognize it at the time, but after replaying the incident back in his mind, he understood why he was on edge. The one blast, which hadn't really been a blast at all, neither a thump nor a bang but more like a "foomp," had been different. Now he heard sirens, and he wondered what had happened.

Avery casually looked in the direction of the bridge construction, and the hair on his back became stiff. He felt a chill run up his spine, and his adrenaline started flowing. An inner voice told him that the "foomp" sound had come from another direction. Avery's six-foot, two-inch frame stood bolt upright. His foot caught the telescope stand as he spun around, and the telescope toppled to the boat deck. He faced the part of the lake where his home and boathouse apartment were located at the entrance of Merrygold Cove. He had to peer through the pine trees growing out on the point, blocking his view.

Carl, who was lying on the padded railing bench listening to the Yankees/Tigers baseball game on his headset, jumped up when the telescope hit the deck, breaking its ten-inch lens. He took one look at his brother's face and knew something was wrong, very wrong indeed. Avery was never one to overreact to anything. He was always cool under pressure, not letting his facial expressions reveal his true thoughts. Carl saw something he'd never seen in his brother's eyes before, fear and anguish. Avery's expression of anxiety frightened Carl.

Avery thought he spotted some flashing red lights reflecting off the lake's calm surface near where his home was. He felt a sense of urgency to get back there now, but his immediate actions were in vain, because the damage had been done almost an hour before. His and Carl's lives would never be the same again.

2

Scotty and Ed had fished the lake together for over thirty years. Despite the prolonged bridge construction, almost every night they were able to get out they were able to catch their limit of walleyed pike by slowly drift fishing the shoreline near the point. They knew the movements of the prized and elusive fish and had developed a sixth sense about how the fish would act on any given night. They also knew that any unusual actions, noises, or disturbances would make catching the pike next to impossible. Scotty had nearly packed it in for the night when the explosion and fire occurred almost directly across the lake from them an hour earlier. They both speculated that some asshole summer renter had forgotten to release the pressure on his rental boat fuel tank and blown the boat—and his ass—to kingdom come when he'd tried to restart the motor.

Scotty snorted and said, "Summer folks are messing the lake up with their trash again, Ed."

Ed didn't say anything, knowing that something like that explosion, which had reached all the way across the lake, might have spooked the fish a little but that they would settle down soon as long as nothing else happened. He poured himself a coffee and prepared to wait the fish out.

Just when things had quieted down and the fish had started taking interest again, that no-good son of a bitch in the big runabout came flying around the point at full throttle, with all his running lights on. He narrowly missed their fourteen-foot aluminum cartop, causing Scotty's new Coleman lantern to fall off the seat and smash in the boat's well. They both knew their fishing was shot for the night and started packing up their gear, cursing all the while.

To make matters worse, the big boat's wake caused the smaller boat to swing backward toward shore, where the outboard's propeller banged up against some rocks, breaking a shear pin. The old motor's propeller went limp and would stay that way until a new pin was inserted. The fishermen would have to row two miles back to the camper because Scotty had the spare shear pins in his other tackle box.

Ed knew this was no time to crack one of his smart-ass jokes and kept his mouth shut. He grabbed the oars and started rowing.

3

Avery cursed while he searched for the ignition key firmly attached to the big lime green fluorescent, guaranteed not to sink, marine key ring. Finding it, he jammed it home, turning over the twin 454-cubic-inch engines.

Carl, meanwhile, busied himself with the anchor. As soon as Avery saw it was clear, he turned all the running light switches on and slammed the throttle full forward. The big boat lurched ahead, causing Carl to lose his balance momentarily. He grabbed the cocaptain's seat to steady himself.

For a moment Carl thought Avery had cut the corner of the point too sharp and they would run up on the rocks. Carl was relieved when he didn't hear that sickening crunch of rock versus almost anything. He was set aback again when Avery veered away at the last moment, narrowly missing two guys in a small fishing boat. Carl thought he saw a light in the fisherman's boat, but when he looked back he didn't see the light or the boat. He worried that they had capsized.

Carl replayed the events of the night over and over again in his mind for weeks. He never recalled the incident with the two fishermen until just before pulling the trigger of the .38 revolver planted firmly against his temple. Carl laughed at how insignificant this memory was compared with everything that had transpired since his wife died. The recent deaths of his daughter and sister-in-law had been too much for him to deal with.

4

Walt Beyer was eagerly getting the VCR and portable television situated on his covered patio where he planned to spend the next four hours or so watching *The History of the Civil War.* His wife had taped it for him the previous week while he was working the night watch at the fire station. Walt's wife, Dianne, and his daughter, Vicki, were out shopping at the new Wal-Mart over in Jamestown, and he intended to watch the entire series without interruption.

He had just returned from the kitchen with a cold beer and was ready to hit the play button on the VCR when Wolf, his two-year-old German pointer, started barking at phantoms down near the lake. Walt knew he would have no peace unless he reassured the dog there were no monsters threatening to come out of the water and terrorize them.

Walt walked the fifty feet or so to where Wolf was having his fit, and the dog stopped barking and started growling. Walt noticed that the dog's back hairs were raised in anticipation of a confrontation. Wolf was looking directly out into the water, where Walt noticed some sort of disturbance, bubbles, about two hundred feet from shore off to the east, but nothing to be overly concerned about.

Walt had had a busy day off, taking care of minor chores around the house. He'd managed to fix the pulley on the boat winch, which would have been a major pain in the ass when the weather turned cold near the end of October and snow threatened. Now he noticed how nice an evening it was.

Looking around, he saw that it was a calm night with little boat traffic out on the lake, except for a few die-hards drift-fishing out near the point across the lake with lanterns in their boats. The night sky was clear and visibility was good, even though there was only a quarter moon. Everyone on this part of the lake seemed to be out on their patios or in their boathouses taking advantage of the warm, late September evening, and the area was lit up like a carnival.

Walt looked over in envy at the Profrock place, where the lights were on in the boathouse apartment. He thought it strange that someone would be there because Avery usually worked up there during the daytime, writing those mystery books, and closed it up at night. Walt mentally kicked himself in the ass again because he had had a chance to buy the place when old man Strasberg had died, but he'd waited too long to make an offer on it. Walt particularly liked the boathouse.

Mr. Strasberg had a thirty-foot custom-built Richardson cruiser, and he'd had the boathouse built from ten-inch steel I beams concreted into the lake bottom under six feet of water. There was a twenty-ton electric hoist to lift the big boat out of the water in winter. Mr. Strasberg stored it there because he didn't like the idea of paying someone else to take care of his baby. When Walt was younger, the other kids had jokingly called it "Old Man Strasberg's steel barn." Looking at it now, Walt realized that was just what it looked like, a big barn. It had steel sheeting welded to the north and west exposures to protect it from the harsh winters. Most of the wooden structures built on the lake were subject to rotting, requiring repairs every spring after the winter ice did its damage.

Walt didn't really feel that bad about missing out on the opportunity, because Avery and Karen were really nice folks. When Vicki had been having a bad time in school, Karen had tutored her every night for a month, and Avery had never let his success go to his head. Avery's brother and his niece Desiree were staying with them, and Walt noticed Karen and Desiree were up in the apartment, laughing. The two were having great fun doing something or other. Walt remembered that Desiree's mother had died about a year ago of cancer, and he felt comfortable knowing Karen was helping the girl deal with her emotional healing.

He turned his attention back to Wolf, reassuring him that there was nothing to be worried about. Walt noticed that whatever it was that had spoofed Wolf earlier was gone, and the dog was back to his usual couldn't-give-a-shit attitude.

Walt headed back to the patio, with the dog faithfully at his side. They were near the end of the path, ready to step up onto the patio, when the night air was shattered by a deafening roar and concussion. The blast threw man and dog across the backyard into a chain-link fence on the other side of the driveway. Walt was shaken but struggled to his feet, knowing immediately that it had been some sort of fuel explosion, with an impact unlike anything he had experienced in twenty years as a fireman. He also knew that Wolf would no longer be chasing phantoms in the night because the dog was dead.

Walt went directly into the house, where he grabbed his home-based radio and called in the emergency to his station. He looked out his broken kitchen window and noticed that it was the Profrocks' place burning. He felt a hollow feeling in the pit of his stomach because the whole lakeside and eastern exposure of the boathouse apartment were gone. Walt had a short memory flash of Karen and Desiree and knew their fate.

Walt grabbed his gear and headed to the site to assist the on-duty station men who would be arriving soon. He heard the sirens before he got to the end of the driveway. He wanted to do something to help, but he knew it would be useless.

5

Captain Highgate left his house as soon as he heard the alarm on his home scanner when Walt Beyer called it in. The captain could see the glow of the fire above the trees before he reached Merrygold Lane and cursed. He knew the new fire-fighting rig would get all scratched up maneuvering the narrow road some three hundred yards to where the fire was. He was already having guilt pangs about his concerns for the rig's paint job knowing that the people whose house was burning couldn't give a rat's ass about a scratched paint job.

He was just beginning to make the left turn onto Merrygold Lane when he caught sight of the other car's headlights just before it slammed into him. The firehouse station wagon spun around and he almost lost it, but he got it straightened out and hit the brakes. He looked back just in time to see two nondescript dark-colored cars leaving the lane and heading east on the main road. They were in a big hurry. Even though the wagon's left rear side was badly damaged and the rear door was sprung open, it was drivable, and he headed toward the fire knowing he would make a report later.

6

Avery powered the big boat directly across the lake toward his home trying to make sense of what he was seeing. He could see what at first looked like a boat burning out on the lake about two hundred feet from shore. There were red flashing emergency lights from the fire-fighting equipment positioned near shore at the entrance of Merrygold Cove. He was sure now that something terrible had happened and felt somewhat relieved when he noticed that the fire-fighting equipment was on the opposite side of the cove. He thought that a boat had exploded near the mouth of the cove and was burning itself out while freely drifting out in the bay. Avery's adrenaline rush decreased and he could feel his muscles release their grip on his shoulders, neck, and back.

He reached over and started backing off on the throttle, slowing the boat down just in case he had to do some quick maneuvering to avoid debris in the water. He was about to reach for the searchlight mounted on the deck just outside the windshield when he heard a strange choking sound coming from Carl. When he looked over at his brother he saw a distorted look of anguish and terror that reminded him of the faces actors make in bad horror movies.

When Avery looked over and saw what had caused Carl's anguish he immediately felt totally sapped of all energy. What he saw reminded him of the dinosaurs in science museums. All that was left of his boathouse apartment was the skeletal remains of the steel I beams with shards of wood trim, drywall, and insulation material dangling from wires and metal stripping. Some of the material was still smoldering and now he understood why the fire-fighting equipment was on the other side of the narrow cove: it was the best angle to pour water on the fire. He thought it odd that the north and west walls of the boathouse were still standing. Avery was well aware of how the mind can play tricks on people, and this was one of those times. He tried to rationalize why the sight of the boathouse in that condition made him think of an old and badly neglected barn but could not rationalize it at all. He looked out into the bay and realized that what he thought to be a boat burning was actually a twelve-by-twenty-foot section of solid oak hardwood flooring he had laid in the apartment himself earlier that spring.

Avery felt a sense of instant urgency when he noticed three things: the house lights were not on, Karen and Desiree were nowhere to be seen, and Walt Beyer had a look of total despair on his face. Walt was looking right into Avery's eyes.

7

Manny Carlyle was back in good spirits since he found out where that no-good son of a bitch rat squealing bastard Jerry Flanigan was being hidden away by the federal marshals awaiting his trail on drug trafficking charges. All Manny had to do was get rid of him and the prosecution's case was out the window, because Manny had already made sure that most of the evidence against him would be thrown out of court. Manny knew the other evidence was worthless without the testimony of Jerry. It cost Manny a lot of money to recruit an inside man, but it was worth it. He had the inside track on the prosecutor's case and with Flanigan out of the way, the case was dead.

Manny felt energized and was porking everything in a skirt again. He spent the evening with some of the most respected citizens of Erie, Pennsylvania, at a fund raiser for homeless and runaway children where he graciously contributed $100,000. After all, it was an investment in the future because these kids were some of his consumers. He wanted to make sure his every move was well documented this evening, so he wouldn't be considered a suspect when the Flanigan family and anyone unfortunate enough to be near them were blown into another star system. He knew his every move was being monitored and decided to put on a show for whoever had the honor of tailing him tonight. He arranged to meet a prominent attorney's young wife at a local motel where he left some lights on in the room so they would get a good focus on their camera.

Manny left the motel and decided to make the phone call that would complete his day. He stopped at a phone booth and dialed another pay phone on the other side of town where one of his men had been waiting for over an hour. The phone hadn't finished its first ring when Petie answered it, saying, "Pete's Hoagie House."

This was Manny's signal that all was clear, and Manny said, "Give me the good news."

Petie hesitated, wishing he didn't have to be the one to tell Manny the bad news, but finally said, "Your steak-and-cheese sub was delivered to the wrong address."

When Manny heard the message he bit down so hard that he broke a cap on one of his teeth. He slammed the phone down into its holder in a rage. His rage would continue until the phone booth was a total shambles. He cursed, wishing that he hadn't let his business partners talk him out of using his own men to take care of that rat-bastard Flanigan. Manny had been uncomfortable from the beginning contracting the job out to those hicks out at the lake. He had a gut feeling that they would fuck it up. He didn't particularly give a shit or not if it looked like an accident; all he wanted was Flanigan dead before he testified. His rage heightened because deep down he wanted to be the one who killed that bastard. He wanted to leave his calling card letting everyone know that he took care of his own problems. It was important in his line of work to let people know who was in charge and what price would be paid for disloyalty. He also knew that contracting out a job like this would let his competition know he was vulnerable, and that made him very uncomfortable.

One of the surveillance men assigned to tail Manny laughed when he saw him trash the phone booth and said to the other, "Manny must have gotten some bad news."

The other replied, "Maybe he got a bill from the babe's lawyer husband for services rendered."

Manny didn't care if his car phone was monitored or not. He made the call to Buffalo to see if his salvage crew could pick up the pieces and find Flanigan's trail again. Manny had no doubts in his mind that Jerry wasn't being held at the safe house anymore. Manny felt a little at ease, because his inside man would find Flanigan for him. He ran his tongue along the spot where he broke a cap and punched the dashboard so hard that half the courtesy lights on the instrument panel blinked out, which only pissed him off the more.

8

Jeff Culpepper had been collecting miniature Oriental figurines since he bought a small jade dolphin in Saigon in 1966 for the equivalent of about $60. He learned shortly afterward that it had a collector value of $2,000. His newest addition to the collection had been delivered today, and he was giving the piece a close inspection under a lighted magnifying glass when he heard the pager sound off in the other room. His wife, Winnie, accustomed to the regular messages, didn't recognize the coded message blinking on the pager screen. She took it into the study for Jeff's attention.

Jeff read the message on the display screen: "Three Blind Mice in Goldylock's Hair."

Jeff immediately understood that there was trouble at Merrygold House. He felt a great sense of relief, because he knew the message let him know that his two men and Flanigan were out of Merrygold House and safe at an alternate site. Jeff knew his gut feeling to have them on alert was correct. He also knew that reacting to his gut feelings and separating the Flanigan family was the right decision also.

Without speaking, Winnie left the study, closing the door behind her. After living with the district director of the Witness Protection Program for over twenty years she knew that a coded message meant business, and Jeff was very good at his business. She went back to the new Avery Profrock book, which had held her spellbound for the last two hours.

Jeff went to his desk and dialed the switching station, where he got a secure line. He pushed the speed dial for Goldylock's, a safe house near the New York–Pennsylvania border where his team leader, who had escaped Merrygold, filled him in on the attempted assassination and that there would be a mess to clean up.

Culpepper had two rules that had helped him survive in this business and become the best there ever was. First rule: there is no such thing as coincidence, neverfuckingever. Second rule: if the feds want their witnesses protected, they clean up any messes. He knew that this explosion at Merrygold was no coincidence, and he knew who to call to clean up the mess. His next call was to agent Bill Trusk in Buffalo.

Bill Trusk thought about protesting the assignment but knew he would be answering to a superior in the morning if he did. After all, Culpepper had a reputation that was hard to go up against. He never lost a protected witness.

With this little problem delegated out to the proper agency, Jeff knew that any mess left at the lake would be taken care of. There would be a lot of official ID flashing, suppression of evidence, and a proper amount of disinformation. Jeff could direct his attention to the other problem at hand: who was feeding information to Manny Carlyle? There were only five people who knew the location of the Flanigan team at the lake. Jeff could rule out four of them because he hadn't let the information out and none of the three men at the house would set themselves up to be blown away. He reflected for a moment on Culpepper rule number one but mentally tossed the notion away, as usual.

Jeff went back to his miniature pondering how he could stay in operation while keeping information away from his supervisor, Franklin Crawley. Jeff wondered if someone else was aware of the location, but it didn't matter because it was compromised now. The safe house would have to be disposed of.

Later that evening, Jeff gave serious thought, for the first time, whether his decision to enter the white man's arena of power and control was a mistake. As a black man, he never questioned his capabilities or confidence. But his suspicions were giving him reason to be concerned.

9

Avery shut off the engines and let the boat ease up to the dock, where Walt Beyer lent a hand with the ropes. As soon as he stepped up to the dock opposite his boathouse, Avery glanced at the small aluminum boat shelter on the east side of the dock and noticed that it was leaning over severely. It was twisted at an awkward angle, and Avery knew that it took a special kind of explosive material to cause concussion impact damage like that. He remembered the old wooden cottage that once sat on this side of the cove and knew that it would have been destroyed by the blast, as well as the old couple who spent their summers there.

Carl sidestepped Avery. He was heading toward the arched overhead pedestrian bridge that connected the two shores of the narrow cove. Walt Beyer intercepted him and forced him onto an old wooden bench. Avery's interest in the old aluminum boat shelter became passé when he spotted Walt and Carl in what looked like a tug-of-war near the old bench. He went over to the bench to see what was going on. When he arrived at the bench he was met by Captain Highgate, who looked Avery straight in the eye and said, "There's something you have to know, Ave: we believe Karen and your niece were in the boathouse when it blew up."

When Walt got Carl calmed down he told Avery what he had seen in the apartment moments before the explosion. He added that they were unable to find Karen or Desiree anywhere.

Avery didn't say anything and walked the few steps toward the water's edge, where he scanned the lake. He could see something still burning out in the bay and a lot of debris scattered everywhere. He looked down and noticed something familiar and picked it up. His heart sank and his eyes welled with tears. He was holding the mouse from his computer with a yellow happy-face sticker on it that Karen had attached that morning in celebration of completing his most recent book.

Dianne Beyer and a couple other neighbors gathered near Avery and Carl to comfort them.

10

Avery awoke thinking he had been having a bad nightmare only to be jolted back to reality when he looked out the window to see a lot of people milling around. He saw the sheriff's underwater rescue boat out in the bay. There was a coroner's wagon parked near the end of the road on the other side of the cove. Two men were sitting on the old bench talking to another man standing directly in front of them. Avery noticed that the man standing was wearing a blue jacket with big letters stenciled on the back reading FBI and wondered why they were there.

Avery heard a noise and when he turned he recognized Dianne Beyer. Dee, to her close friends, had a very large mug of steaming coffee in her hand as she walked over to Avery. She set the mug down and gave Avery an embrace that communicated more than words could possibly do. Dee informed Avery that she had contacted his agent about what had happened and that he would be arriving this afternoon to help with anything he could. She told Avery that Carl was still asleep in the guest room. She also told Ave that she had contacted the Dubois Funeral Home and Bob would make all the arrangements.

Avery tried to thank Dee, but when he opened his mouth to say the words nothing came out. Dee told him it was OK. He put on his weathered denim jacket, grabbed the mug of coffee, and went outside.

Avery walked toward the back of the boathouse. Looking at it, he realized that if it wasn't for the broken windows you wouldn't think there was anything wrong. He noticed two men fixing the gate on the chain-link fence of the house next to his boathouse. He wondered how the explosion had damaged it, because everything on the west side of the boathouse was relatively intact. His attention was diverted again when he saw Walt Beyer and Captain Highgate on the other side of the road in a heated discussion. Avery noticed that they were really pissed off about something. He walked over to the two men, and as soon as he got near they broke off the discussion and simultaneously asked Avery if he was OK. When he assured the two men that he was fine, he learned that they were angry about being kept away from the fire scene by the FBI. They had taken control of the investigation. It seemed they believed some of the explosives from the bridge construction site had gotten loose and drifted down to Avery's place and blown up the boathouse. Avery thought about what the captain had said and turned to walk back to the boathouse but couldn't help noticing the damage to the captain's new station wagon. Captain Highgate had noticed Avery's interest in the wagon and said, "That reminds me; I got nailed out by the main road last night when I was responding to the alarm. I'll have to file a report. Those two cars were in a big hurry and didn't even think about stopping after hitting me." Avery glanced back over at the two men fixing the chain-link fence and again wondered how it got damaged.

He walked back to the boathouse and looked through one of the broken windows just in time to see two black plastic body bags being loaded in the coroner's wagon. Dee, who was watching from the kitchen window, got to Avery just before his legs turned to Jell-O and his lights went out. With the help of Walt and Captain Highgate, Dee got Avery back into the house.

When Avery came to the next morning the investigation was completed and the boathouse was gone, totally gone.

11

Agent in charge Bill Trusk from the Buffalo office couldn't believe his luck when he got to the lake to clean up the mess. He discovered that explosives were being used on a daily basis for bridge construction. All he had to do was arrange for some explosive materials to be found at the Profrock place similar to the stuff being used at the construction site, and he would be home for the weekend. The official report was signed, sealed, and delivered.

Headlines in the local newspaper read: "Noted Author's Wife and Niece Perish When Loose Dynamite Explodes at Lakeside Home."

Trusk even arranged for the remaining structure of the boathouse to be declared unsafe. All remnants of the boathouse were cut up and hauled away before day's end. He knew Culpepper was a pain in the ass and if a thorough cleanup job wasn't done he would make Trusk go back and do it right. When Trusk submitted the final accidental death report to the insurance company and local municipality he was confident that he had done a complete job.

12

Corry Phillips had been Avery's publishing agent from the beginning and considered himself a part of the family. He knew Avery had no family other than his brother and when he heard about Karen's death he immediately cleared his calendar. He made arrangements to go to his friend's side and help any way he could.

When Corry learned shortly after arriving at the Profrock house that Avery's newest manuscript had been lost in the explosion and fire, he had the unpleasant task of finding someone to retrieve Avery's computer from somewhere on the lake bottom. Corry knew it would be a long shot but hoped the manuscript disc was still intact in the computer. There was only one underwater salvage company in the area, and he contracted them to search the area. Corry was pleased when the computer and disc were recovered, not because he would be able to publish the book, but because the people at the salvage company were sleazy characters. Corry did not want to have to deal with them on a long-term basis. He had a bad feeling about them and gladly paid the thousand-dollar fee to be rid of them. Corry had no way of knowing that the same people he hired to retrieve the manuscript tape were the ones who had killed his friend's wife and niece.

After the funeral Corry flew back to LA, spending the entire flight thinking about Ave and wondering if he would ever get another manuscript from him. Corry knew Avery had an incredible talent for writing. He had the ability to write a 400-page novel from a single thought or observation. Avery was capable of creating bizarre circumstances whereby people in his books met terrible deaths, which led Corry to believe Avery had an underlying evil side to him and he kept it in check at all times. After reading one of Avery's best-sellers, a colleague remarked, "This Profrock fellow writes like Hawthorne incarnate."

Corry remembered the look in Avery's eyes when he left and knew he would need a lot of time to get over Karen's death, if, in fact, he ever could get over it.

13

Bob DuBois had a reputation in the mortuary science business as being the best there was at reconstructing cadavers for open-casket funerals, but the damage to Karen Profrock and her niece was beyond his expertise. He knew that this would be one of the biggest funerals of his career and regretted not being able to provide a proper service for the family. He had genuine respect for all the people he prepared for their final resting place and went to great lengths in preserving their dignity. He knew that if he ever became desensitized by his work he would find another business. Unquestionably, he knew that preparing the young girl's body for shipment to Naples, Florida, for her funeral was the most difficult thing he had ever done.

14

A month after the funeral Avery was beginning to come out of the stupor that had kept him caught in an emotional Ping-Pong game since the accident. He started regaining some semblance of normalcy and decided to take care of the things that had been neglected. When he checked the mail he realized that Dee had paid the utility bills and kept food in the house. He vaguely remembered writing checks and, looking around the house, realized that Dee had been taking care of everything. He walked over to the dining room table, where he noticed a small mountain of sympathy cards. He found other letters from insurance companies, and that sort, neatly separated and stacked. He peeked into the bedroom, and for the life of him he couldn't remember making the bed. He realized that Dee had been holding down the fort while he was off on a mental voyage somewhere—a place where it was foggy, cold, and lonely, but he was never really alone.

He recalled returning from a walk the week before and finding Dee crying by the back door. When Avery approached her she didn't say anything; she just got in the car and drove away. Avery felt a sudden stab of guilt because it had just occurred to him that Dee was going to dispose of Karen's clothes and other belongings that morning. He realized it must have been a very difficult task for her.

When the phone rang, distracting him from his thoughts, he let it ring, knowing the answering machine would announce his absence. He would get the message later. He recognized Walt Beyer's voice on the machine. Walt had a reserved hesitation in his message, and he wanted to talk to Avery. He asked Avery to please come to the house this evening, saying it was important.

25

Karen hadn't indulged in many personal comforts except for her small collection of antique dolls. She had a porcelain Korean doll she had named Kathy. Of the forty dolls in Karen's collection, Kathy was her favorite. Avery knew that the doll would have a special meaning to Dee and decided to take it with him later when he went to see Walt. He walked over to the phone and replayed Walt's message. When he heard it again Avery read something into it.

"Avery, this is Walt. . . . I got something I need to talk to you about. . . . It's, ah, well, ah, it's important, I think. Anyway, stop by the house tonight and I'll tell you about it."

Avery went back to the pile of sympathy cards and spent the afternoon going through them. He knew the healing process would take a very long time.

15

When Avery arrived at Walt and Dee's house he felt a sense of uneasiness in the room and apologized if he had come at a bad time. He said he could come back later, but Walt insisted he stay. Dee looked at Avery and said that Walt had something to talk to him about, against her better judgment, but she reluctantly agreed that he had a right to know what it was. Dee added, "I just don't think this is the right time for you to have to deal with what Walt has to say."

Avery gently placed his hand on her shoulder and said, "Walt is not one to trivialize, and if he has something to tell me that is causing friction between the two of you, it must be important, and I should know what it is." He handed Dee the Kathy doll and said, "Karen would have wanted you to have this."

Dee gently embraced the doll and silently drifted into the living room, leaving Walt and Avery in the kitchen to take care of business.

Avery sat down at the kitchen table while Walt, aware that he had never seen Avery drink alcohol, returned from the counter with a bottle of Jim Beam and two glasses. Walt had a paper lunch bag that clanked when he set it down on the Formica-covered table. Walt sat down directly across from Avery and mentally gathered his thoughts before speaking. It was a comfortable night, but Avery couldn't help but noticing that there were beads of sweat forming on Walt's forehead. Avery knew his friend was having a very difficult time getting out whatever was bothering him. Avery broke the ice by asking, "What's in the bag, Walt?"

Walt sighed and reached into the bag and handed Avery a piece of metal the size of a car's brake pedal. Avery examined it and noted that it looked like it had been ripped from whatever it was originally attached to and had rough edges. The piece was not jagged except for one side that seemed to have been part of a welded seam. The metal was scorched and distorted, but Avery detected a small amount of white paint that looked familiar, but Avery couldn't immediately identify it. There was something else not quite right about it, and after a closer look he set it back on the table, suspecting Walt would be filling in the gaps.

Walt sat patiently while Avery examined the metal and when he was done started to explain why he had asked him to come over. Avery listened as Walt retraced his and Captain Highgate's examination of the boathouse the morning after the fire looking for anything that might give them a clue to what caused the explosion. They had been gathering materials and were in the process of placing them in plastic bags and tagging them. Then the FBI showed up and took charge of the investigation with their own specialists. Before Captain Highgate could protest they were ushered away from the scene and ordered to stay clear.

Avery remembered seeing Walt and the captain on the other side of the road the morning after the fire and understood why they were so pissed off. He also remembered seeing the two black body bags being loaded into the coroner's wagon just before his legs turned to Jell-O and his lights went out.

Walt hesitated a moment, then continued by saying that he and the captain had decided to let the FBI have their way. They would return the next day and continue their own investigation, but when they came back everything was gone, including the steel I-beam framing. There was nothing left to examine except this piece of metal that Walt unconsciously placed in his fireman's coat pocket. Walt forgot he had put it there and didn't discover it until ten days ago. Walt explained to Avery that he and the captain decided to send the metal sample and a pack of Polaroid pictures they took of the gutted-out boathouse to a friend of theirs who was an explosives expert with the Army Corps of Engineers. They asked him to run some tests on the sample and to keep it confidential.

Walt stopped here and pointed at the piece of metal on the

table and said, "That's a piece of one of the hundred-pound propane tanks stored in the boathouse and used to heat the apartment."

Avery picked up the piece and reexamined it more closely. His stomach suddenly knotted up and ached. Walt grabbed the bottle of whiskey and poured himself an old-fashioned north-eastern four-finger shot before saying, "Our explosive-expert friend decided to run some chemical tests on the metal to find out what could have caused the piece to become bent inward. He found traces of a high-grade plastic explosive, possibly C-4. He also took a good look at the pictures we sent along and said that whoever decided that this was an accidental dynamite explosion doesn't know shit about explosives. He also added that someone would have had to accidentally and simultaneously activate the primers on an entire case of TNT for it to have had that effect. Conclusion: no accident."

Walt poured himself another shot and, after seeing the expression on Avery's face, poured him one, too. Avery placed the piece of metal back on the table and snapped the whiskey down quickly. It burned his throat and tasted bad but cleared his head.

Walt lowered his voice, saying, "Two things have been bothering me, Avery. Who would do something like this? And how did the FBI get involved so fast?"

Avery sat motionless while his mind's eye gave him fast-forward replays of the night his wife and niece died. It was all spinning around in his head and became very confusing, because Walt's last two questions reverberated like an echo over and over again in his ears: *Who would do something like this? And how did the FBI get involved so fast?* He thought he was about to pass out when the sounds of Walt's retching in the bathroom brought him around. Walt was somewhat short and stocky, but very strong. Avery knew his being sick was not a result of being weak; on the contrary, Avery considered him the kind of person you'd want standing in your corner when push came to shove.

Before Avery left the Beyer house he instructed Walt and Dee to keep what they knew to themselves until he had a chance to think it over. He wanted to think about what he was going to do with the information. He got assurance from Walt that the captain had no interest in pursuing the matter, because he had had a visit from some official types with orders to cooperate totally and completely. Captain Highgate was too near retirement to get involved in some bureaucratic bullshit now and wanted to forget the whole thing.

When Avery got home he sat in silent darkness in his den for a long time, trying to make sense of what Walt had told him. It was two in the morning when he got the big flashlight out of the closet and went out to where his boathouse used to be. He didn't know what he expected to find but knew that sleep would elude him tonight. There was a place deep inside his subconscious that told him to get off his ass and do something.

16

The neighbors' seven-foot-high chain-link fence ran along the property line right up to the back of their boathouse. Avery mused at his thinking of them as neighbors, because he rarely saw anybody there. He often thought of asking the guy who maintained the property to consider doing his lawn and other chores. One day when Avery entered the gate to talk to him, the guy told him it was private property and he would have to leave immediately. Avery understood that some people did not want their privacy invaded and apologized to the maintenance man, then left without stating his intentions. He didn't want problems with his neighbors. He remembered mentioning the incident to Walt the next day and Walt laughed because he, too, had tried to introduce himself but was informed that the property was owned by a manufacturing company in Jamestown. He had learned that the house was only used when the company executives and engineers came to conduct business away from the office. Avery could relate to that because he couldn't work on his books unless he isolated himself. He had built the boathouse apartment for just that reason. That also explained why the people he did see there on rare occasions were dressed fashionably casual. It also helped explain why people only came to the house late at night and usually left before daylight. He noticed for the first time that there was a FOR SALE sign attached to the gate with the realtor's name and phone number.

Avery worked his way to the boathouse and was glad to see that the narrow wooden ledge was still in place. He squeezed his way down the ledge but discovered the window was too high to shine his light in. Avery noticed it would be useless anyway, because the glass in the window was frosted, and thought it strange he never noticed this before. He continued down the ledge to the end and peeked around the corner of the boathouse lake entrance. Avery cursed under his breath because the door was lowered to water level and it had no windows. He turned to go back and snagged his sleeve on something. He eased his sleeve loose and examined what looked like a thumbtack with a small piece of plastic yellow ribbon attached to it. He removed the thumbtack and took a closer look at the ribbon. He thought he should know what it was but it escaped his memory. He stuck it in his pocket. Avery realized that if he wanted to look inside he would have to go over the fence to the other side of the L-shaped house, which was attached to the boathouse. He still didn't know what he was looking for, and before he gave his action any thought he was over the fence and rounding the house.

Avery was not aware that he had tripped several silent alarms that alerted the private security company monitoring station. It seemed to be a night of new discoveries for Avery, because when he got to the far side of the house he noticed that there was a high wooden stockade fence running the full length of the property line. Barbed wire was strung along its length, and he realized that the house could not be seen from the lake. He stored this new information back in the "let's look at it later in the light of day" part of his brain and went directly to the boathouse window on the back side of the house. He shined his light in.

The boathouse contained the normal collection of stuff that one would associate with a boathouse, including a boat hook hanging from a nail on the wall, a couple of coiled ropes, and some bumper rail pads. Nothing out of the ordinary. He panned the light toward where the doorway to the house should be. He had to press his face up against the window in an awkward way just to get a sliver of a glimpse. Hard as he tried, he couldn't see enough to satisfy his curiosity. He noticed that a tall, narrow window located where the hallway between the boathouse and the house entrance would be was slightly ajar. He shined his light into it and saw a 100-pound propane tank in the corner of the hallway right next to the door leading into the house. Avery realized that the window was left open for ventilation, and when he shined the light higher he saw that the tank was full, according to the gauge. He heard a humming noise above and shined the light a little higher to discover a small ventilation fan working its little heart out. He wondered if the little fan was hooked up to a timer as his was. He shined the light along the electrical conduit and saw that it led to a switch that was designed to be tripped when the boathouse door was closed. Avery appreciated the safety features of the system because he knew firsthand how volatile propane can be. He shined the light back in the narrow window in the direction of the fan and noticed something stuck in the fan's protective grate. Avery had to squint to see what it was. When he recognized it as a piece of yellow plastic ribbon like the kind police use to rope off an accident or crime scene, a memory came crashing into his mind.

The night of the "accident" (he knew now that it was no accident) Avery had been backing the boat out of the boathouse for a night of stargazing when he noticed Carl leaning over the left side of the boat trying to grab something blowing in the breeze. It was a length of plastic yellow ribbon, and when Carl broke it loose from the neighbors' boathouse he lost his grip on it. The ribbon got hung up on a piece of splintered wood on the side of Avery's boathouse. Avery took a wild stab at it, but it was out of his reach. He saw Carl laughing lightheartedly, and Avery felt good because it was the first time he had seen Carl laugh since Nancy died. Avery also remembered that when he headed out into the lake there was an underwater recovery boat setting up for what appeared to be a night dive about a thousand yards out in the lake off to the east. Avery remembered Carl asking him what they would be looking for at night. Avery didn't know at the time, but he knew now. They were a demolition team, and the plastic yellow ribbon was their target marker.

Avery's mind was racing and he was deep in thought, but his concentration was broken when he saw a searchlight shining against the tall wooden fence with the barbed wire on top. He froze in his tracks, waiting to be discovered, because he had nowhere to go. He was starting to put together a good story for whoever was bound to find him when a large black dog dashed down the fence and out a small opening at the other end. Avery heard someone laugh and speak to someone else, saying, "It's just a dog. Tell Central to call off the alert and turn off those sensors. Nobody lives here anymore. What a pain in the ass."

Avery waited a short time before returning to his house. He looked over his shoulder at the house where nobody lived anymore and wondered if anyone ever really had lived there. He went into his house, where someone sort of lived.

17

When the morning-newspaper boy dropped the paper in Avery's back door and let the door slam shut Avery woke in a start, jumping to his feet. When he saw the boy out of the side window he settled down but was shaking and remembered a dream, a dream where he was searching for Karen in a cold, smoky warehouse. He couldn't figure out why it was cold, because the entire building was on fire. He could hear Karen calling for him, but he couldn't get to her. In the dream he was being held back by long strips of plastic yellow ribbon hanging down from the ceiling. When he tried to move them out of the way he kept getting hung up on thousands of thumbtacks sticking out of the ribbon. He had grabbed a huge oversize boat hook and started separating the ribbon strips when there was a gigantic explosion and that's when the door slamming shut woke him up.

Still shaking, Avery went over and retrieved the paper and threw it on the kitchen table. He made a pot of strong coffee, knowing he would need it. He went to the bathroom and brushed his teeth and shaved while thinking. Avery had a very large question that needed answering, and he mentally made the question as big as possible so he would focus on it: WHY?

Before getting himself a coffee, he went to the den and grabbed a large lined yellow writing pad and wrote: "WHY????" on the top of the pad in large letters. He knew if he could answer the why, he would have a good chance of finding out who.

He went to the counter and poured himself a coffee, then settled at the table, where he started making a "To Do" list:

- Find out who owned the house that nobody lived in with ground sensors, private security, barbed-wire fences, and frosted boathouse windows.
- Find out what the underwater salvage people were doing out in the lake that night.
- Find out why the FBI got involved and who was behind them. (Be very careful checking this out, Ave.)
- Get Walt and Dee a new dog!

Avery decided that the first thing on the list could be accomplished this morning and grabbed the paper to find the real estate listings. When he picked up the paper his eye caught the bottom of the front-page headline reading: "TWO LOCAL UNDERWATER SALVAGE WORKERS FOUND SHOT." He read the article and learned that both men had been found shot to death, execution style, in the trunk of an abandoned car near the salvage-company yard.

Avery flipped to the obituary section and read that one of the men found in the car had served four years in the navy and was a Seabee. Avery thought about this for a moment and added to the list of things to do:

- Find out who or what the two dead salvage men knew that got them killed.

He went to the coatrack and reached in the pocket of his jacket and pulled out the thumbtack with a small piece of plastic yellow ribbon. He added to the list:

- Find out where one gets plastic ribbon and who tacked it to the boathouse connected to the house where nobody lived less than three feet from my boathouse.

Avery then added one more thing to his list:

- If anyone associated with Karen and Desiree's death isn't already dead, consider the options.

He then read the real estate write-up about the house that nobody lived in and called them for a showing. The agent who took the call said she would be out to give him a tour in about three hours.

Avery went to the kitchen and made a breakfast big enough for four men and spent the rest of the morning finishing the small mountain of sympathy cards and other mail. When he found a copy of the official accident report he added another thing to his "To Do" list:

- Find out who agent Bill Trusk is and why he falsified his report.

Avery thought about his bull-in-the-china-shop tactics the night before while checking out the neighbors' house and how his recklessness had summoned the security patrol. He made a mental pledge not to make small mistakes like that again, because the people he was going after—and yes, he was going after them—were the type who had little respect for human life. These people were the type who did not negotiate but dealt with problems in a violent, lethal, and permanent fashion. He suddenly had a mental image of his father, who had died over fifteen years ago. When he buried Avery Sr. he also buried a well-kept secret.

Before Avery Sr. died of cancer, he and his elder son had spent three years ridding society of the worst of criminal types. Avery was alone in the house but could have sworn that someone nudged him in the back. He remembered the child rapist/murderer who had mysteriously disappeared the day after his father's funeral, never to be seen again. Avery often wondered if anyone ever picked up on these details in his books.

Avery Sr. had spent over twenty frustrating years in the New York Police Department and lived his last three years in pain due to his illness, but he died a happy man. Carl never understood how a man as sick as his father, and in so much pain, could lie on his deathbed with that silly grin on his face.

18

Heather March drove the agency-leased Cadillac up to the gate at Merrygold Lane. She had had exclusive use of the car since topping the agency sales record the previous year. She unlocked the gate and was heading for the house for her showing when the tall man wearing jeans and a faded denim jacket suddenly appeared behind her and she stepped back somewhat startled. She reached in her jacket pocket for the small can of Mace she had kept with her ever since being robbed at an automated teller machine earlier that year.

Avery suddenly realized that he had startled the young lady and apologized to her while introducing himself. Heather looked at him quizzically and glanced behind him as he informed her that he hadn't driven here because he lived there and pointed to his house. Heather released her grip on the potent little weapon and regained her composure. She apologized in return and introduced herself. She smiled but felt awkward and couldn't find anything to say.

Avery broke the ice, smiling, saying, "Well, you going to show me the house, or are we going to stand out here the rest of the afternoon scaring each other?"

Heather laughed and headed toward the house while beginning her sales pitch explaining that the house was privately owned by a manufacturing company in Jamestown. They were selling it because they had no further use for it and were eager to sell. She continued by extolling the security features and stopped when she realized that Avery lived less than three hundred feet away. She realized he would be well aware of the house's exterior and fished the keys out of her purse. Heather unlocked the door and stepped into the house. She turned on all the lights even though it was a bright, cloudless day.

Heather walked down the hallway and stopped at the small kitchen, where Avery took special interest looking for anything out of the ordinary. The first thing he spotted was a high chair in the corner of the room. They continued down the hall to check out the bedrooms. Avery went into the smallest of the three and wondered to himself why a house that was only used for business meetings by executives and engineers would have three bedrooms. He was especially interested why this room had Sesame Street wallpaper and a small bed with a Cinderella bedspread on it.

Heather noticed Avery taking interest in the decor and informed him, "Of course, the house comes completely furnished and the grounds weekly maintenance contract is paid to the end of the year." She took the next sales pitch move, asking, "Are you renting on the lake and interested in buying? If so, this is an excellent buy and won't be on the market for long. The asking price is well below current market value and there are several buyers ready to make offers now."

Avery didn't say anything as he continued his examination of the house. He headed toward the back door to the boathouse. He tried to open the door, but it was locked, and Heather unlocked it for him saying, "This is one of the great features of the house, a private boathouse capable of housing a very large boat and equipment."

Avery examined the steel fire door, keeping silent. He checked the large propane tank against the wall and noticed something he wasn't able to see the night before. He spotted a sign on the wall that read: "TO ALL SOUTHEAST GAS EMPLOYEES. MAKE SURE THAT THE WINDOW ACROSS THE HALL IS OPEN AND THE BOATHOUSE DOOR IS CLOSED AND THE EXHAUST FAN IS OPERATING BEFORE FILLING TANK!" Avery noticed that the sign was covered by a piece of clear plastic and the corners of the plastic were held in place by thumbtacks. Then he noticed that one of the thumbtacks was missing. Avery jammed his hand into his coat pocket and stuck his finger a good one. He pulled the thumbtack out of his pocket and matched it to the ones on the wall. They all had green caps. He put the thumbtack back where it came from, and it went easily into the hole. He reached up and pulled the small piece of yellow plastic ribbon from the exhaust fan grate and stared at the little fan still working its heart out. Before going back to the kitchen Avery looked at the tag attached to the propane tank and saw that it had been filled last week and initialed by PTB. The last time it was filled was on the day of the explosion and fire and it was initialed by JAF. Avery went into the kitchen and got a tall glass of water, and Heather noticed his finger bleeding.

Heather walked over to Avery and said, "You're bleeding. Here, let me look at it." She took his hand and looked at the bleeding finger and went to the bathroom and found a Band-Aid and went back to the kitchen.

Avery said, "Thanks. I must have jabbed it on a splinter in the boathouse. I'm especially interested in it because I need a place to store my boat since the explosion and fire."

Heather looked at Avery, suddenly realizing who he was and what had happened to him not too long ago, and said, "I'm so sorry, I didn't realize, but I should have recognized you when you told me your name and where you lived. You must think me insensitive and rude. And to think I almost gave you a shot of Mace. Please accept my apology and deepest sympathy. I feel like such a fool."

Avery put up his hand to stop her and said, "Thank you, please don't feel embarrassed. It's over and how could you know?" He walked over to the hallway door, and closing it he lied, saying, "I am interested in making an offer on this property. But I would like to have a complete history of it, including the construction order and financial history. Could that be arranged? Of course, I would be willing to pay for any expenses incurred in obtaining this information."

Heather studied Avery for a moment, feeling a little guilty because she unexpectedly found herself sexually drawn to him and wondered if it was because of compassion. She remembered reading about the accident that had killed the local author's wife and niece, and meeting him like this, the way he was dressed and all—well, it wasn't her mental image of him at all. He was not at all what she mentally pictured an author would look like. She suddenly flushed a little and again felt a stab of guilt because she knew the anguish he must be going through. She gathered herself and told him, "That shouldn't be a problem, Mr. Profrock, and I can get the information you need, but it will take a week or two."

Avery could sense that she was sizing him up and felt a little uneasy because he found himself enjoying it in a perverted sort of way. He immediately thought of Karen, and his attention was slammed back into perspective. He started walking toward the door and said, "Please, let's not be so formal. My friends call me Ave, and yes, the information I need is not that important, but I would like to have it before I make an offer on the property. Is a deposit required in the meantime?"

Heather followed Avery to the door, where she turned off the lights before locking it. She stopped Avery saying, "Please accept my apology again. I want to be honest with you and to tell the truth, real estate sales on the lake are terrible recently because of the bridge construction and there aren't any people waiting to make offers. The price, however, is way below true market value and it is a bargain. And no, a deposit is not required until you make an offer."

Avery nodded and walked her to her car, thanking her for being truthful, even though he was well aware of the slumping sales and rentals on the lake all this season. He suddenly felt guilty about deceiving this very attractive woman, using her to do his research for him. He decided that he would make it up to her sometime in the future, and yes, he did have a future again, and a purpose.

He closed and locked the gate for Heather, and as she got in her car she said, "I'll get that information for you as soon as possible and contact you when it's ready."

Avery watched Heather drive off and realized he hadn't given her his unlisted telephone number, but he knew he would see her again, soon. As he walked toward his house he thought of Karen, Desiree, his father, and Carl and decided to call Carl when he got home to see how he was doing. Avery would soon learn that people who successfully shoot themselves in the temple with .38 revolvers don't answer the phone.

At the same time Avery was entering his house, Jeff Culpepper was examining the shell casings that littered the floor of Goldylock's House, knowing that people who were shot repeatedly with a nine-millimeter automatic didn't use the phone either, and he was very upset. Seven people were dead, including three of his best men. The federal prosecutors' office was already demanding a full investigation into the killings, and Culpepper knew he was in for a hard time. Jeff continued examining the murder scene and before long realized that Manny Carlyle had been here. Manny left his personal calling card by shooting everyone with a .45 automatic under the chin. Jeff knew that Manny never could have gotten to the Flanigan family without inside help. He also knew that whoever had made this killing possible would also leave him holding the bag. Jeff realized that he would be held totally responsible for this incident and the prosecutors' office would demand an agency sacrifice.

19

Avery entered the house and had poured himself a cup of coffee when he noticed his answering machine light blinking. He walked over to the machine and hit the PLAY button.

Carl's voice seemed normal, but Avery sensed something was wrong. He listened to the message: "Ave, this is Carl. I just wanted to call and see how things were going. Things haven't changed much around here and I keep myself busy at the investment office. Your investments are doing well and I just sent you a report. If you're not too busy, please give me a call. By the way, I ran into Helen Shepler the other day and she asked me to—" The message ended before Carl finished. Avery cursed, wishing he had programmed the machine to allow the callers more time to finish their message.

Avery knew something was wrong because Carl hated answering machines. He usually left short messages, and this one was too long, and it rambled. Avery replayed the message and detected a strange clicking noise in the background and wondered if Carl had called from his office. He decided to call Carl and see if everything was all right. He dialed the number while fighting a queasy feeling in his stomach and waited. The phone rang three times and Carl's answering machine chimed in: "I'm not available now and I apologize for that. Leave a message and I'll get back to you soon. Please wait for the tone."

Avery waited for the tone and then started to leave a message: "Carl, it's me. I just wanted to return your call and see how yo—" The phone was picked up and Avery felt relieved, but when a stranger's voice said, "Hello. Who is this?" Avery's stomach knotted up again.

Avery hesitated a moment, then said, "My name is Avery Profrock. Whom am I speaking to?"

There was a moment of silence, and then the person on the other end of the line said, "One moment please, Mr. Profrock."

While waiting, Avery could hear a small conversation in hushed voices. After a while someone came on the line and said, "Mr. Profrock, I'm Lieutenant Stephenson of the Naples, Florida, Police Department." There was a short pause, and then Lieutenant Stephenson asked, "Are you related to Mr. Carl Profrock?"

Avery felt acid rising in his throat and thought he was going to be sick. He composed himself and said, "Yes, I'm Carl's brother."

Lieutenant Stephenson held the phone to his chest and crossed himself like a good Catholic should. He gathered his thoughts and said, "Mr. Profrock, would it be possible for you to come to your brother's house? There's been an . . . an accident."

Avery felt anger envelop him like a fog. He didn't like the way the word accident was being used much too loosely lately. He waited until his anger subsided and then answered, "No, Lieutenant. I'm calling from New York. Please tell me what's wrong."

Stephenson told Avery that neighbors had heard what sounded like a gunshot and called the police. When they arrived they discovered Carl in the kitchen. He had apparently committed suicide by a self-inflicted gunshot to the head. Lieutenant Stephenson expressed his deepest sympathy and regrets at having to inform Avery of the tragedy, then asked Avery, "Is there anyone in the Naples area that I can contact for you?"

Avery told the lieutenant that there were no other living relatives. He also informed the lieutenant that he would come to Florida immediately and take care of formalities.

Avery hung up the phone, and the nausea overtook him in a violent manner. He silently grieved the loss of Karen, Desiree, and now Carl.

After a while Avery called Dee Beyer and told her what had happened. He asked her to keep an eye on the house while he was gone.

When Avery returned from Florida he learned that Mr.

Robillesky, who owned the aluminum boat shelter that was damaged by the explosion, had died of a heart attack while trying to fix it. Avery wondered how many more people would suffer directly or indirectly because of the explosion and fire. He also wondered who or what could be worth it. Avery would learn some time later that the entire Flanigan family and three federal marshals died the same day as Carl.

20

Jeff Culpepper was leaving a meeting with his supervisor and a senior member of the federal prosecutors' office at the same time Avery was leaving the cemetery. The funeral service had been attended by several people from Carl's investment company and some neighbors.

Culpepper, in a way, felt like he had just left a funeral, his own. He had been removed from duty while an investigation was under way to determine whether neglect of duty had contributed to the deaths of the three marshals and the Flanigan family. Jeff did not make an official objection to the suspension because he was unable to link anyone else in the agency to the killings. Except for his two men, Flanigan and Crawley, Jeff was the only person who had known that the Flanigan family would be separated at Merrygold house. Knowing this, he decided to keep a close eye on the Goldylock's location after the incident at Merrygold. He kept that information away from everybody, especially Franklin Crawley. Jeff couldn't figure out how the location was leaked out and for a while considered freeing Crawley of suspicion. Before leaving his office for the meeting with Crawley and the senior prosecutor, he checked his computer message file and noticed two user records that were not his. His interest was piqued when he saw that these entries were timed and dated the night before the killings at Goldylock's. Jeff used a complicated password combination that he thought nobody could access unless they had his office bugged and checked it regularly to assure security. He decided to check the computer-logged telephone entries that were recorded from his office phone. He noticed that two calls were made on the same night his password was bastardized and ordered a printout of the numbers. He retrieved the printout and recognized one of the numbers as Goldylock's. The other number was not local, and he picked up his phone and punched it in.

The phone rang several times, and Jeff was about to hang up, deciding to run a trace on the number later, when someone answered it saying, "Hello," in a sheepish tone.

Jeff asked, "Who is this?"

The person on the other end of the phone said, "I'm Randy. Who is this?"

Jeff introduced himself without letting the other person know who he really was and asked, "Where is your phone located?"

Randy replied, "It's on the corner of Tenth and Canal Street, ah, a phone booth...in Erie, PA. What can I do for you?"

Jeff almost hung up again but asked Randy, "Look around and tell me what's near you."

Randy started giving Jeff an inventory of his surroundings. "There's a wire trash can, a bar behind me, a couple of small stores on this corner, a drugstore, and a restaurant across the street. Why?"

Jeff suspected he was reaching for straws but asked Randy to give him the names of the businesses anyway.

Randy said, "Sure, it's your quarter. Let's see, there's Carny's, Buffalo Bob's, K's Boutique, and across the street there's Hasting's RX. And next to that is Pete's Hoagie House. Does that help ya any?"

Jeff silently said, *Bingo.* He recognized Pete's Hoagie House as one of Manny Carlyle's so-called legitimate businesses from an FBI profile. He asked Randy if he was a good guy or a bad guy.

Randy said, "I'm a good guy and I think you are, too."

Jeff said, "Good, because you just gave me some information that will help me get rid of some very bad guys indeed."

Randy was silent for a moment and then said, "Yeah, I know who owns Pete's place, too. If you're going after that scuzzy bastard Carlyle, I'm glad I could help. Good luck, pal, but be careful."

47

Jeff hung up the phone. Smiling slyly, he went to his meeting thinking he would have to find out how Crawley got his computer password and code. He also knew he was set up beautifully and understood that nothing good was going to come from his meeting with Crawley.

Jeff left the meeting knowing that if he wanted to prove Franklin Crawley was behind the killings he would have to go to the lake. He was impressed with the thorough cleanup job Bill Trusk had done at the lake but wasn't sure if he could approach him with his suspicions.

Jeff decided that a long-overdue vacation was in order, a semiworking vacation where he and Winnie could get in some early skiing.

Jeff would never find out how Crawley accessed his computer system.

21

Manny knew that his associates understood completely that he was going to step up the cocaine distribution operation along the entire East Coast from the Florida Keys to Hudson Bay in northern Canada. His associates' diplomatic immunity, although valued, was no longer a necessity. Manny's recent success in ridding himself of Jerry Flanigan and having all federal charges dropped due to insufficient evidence, and no witnesses to testify against him, gave him total freedom. His new man in Washington had access to everything that could pose a threat to him, and nothing stood in his way.

The foreign diplomats' children knew that their immunity presented ideal situations for them to deliver drugs all over the world with little fear of ramifications. The financial rewards were unlike anything they could realize under normal circumstances, and Manny recruited them very carefully. As long as Manny had a need for their immunity they all knew they were valuable and he took very good care of them. They understood now that their diplomatic immunity would not protect them from Manny, who was feeling more invincible than ever. Shortly after their meeting with Manny they all returned to their native countries, never to return.

Manny was gloating over his success in getting rid of Flanigan and arranging for the disposal of the three idiots at the lake. His recent agreement with the South Americans was solidified after he assured them that his man in Washington would keep him totally informed and the cocaine distribution operation would run smoothly. He was finally where he wanted to be, and those who had competed with him were now employees. Manny could now settle old scores at his leisure, and he was very happy with his new power. He was planning his next move toward the top and feeling confident that nobody stood in his way. However, Manny had no idea whatsoever that his man in Washington was negotiating his own deal with the South Americans and Manny would soon be expendable. He was also totally ignorant to the fact that a widowed mystery writer and a displaced civil servant were coming after him. His man in Washington was in serious trouble also.

22

Avery often noticed Southeast Gas Company service vans parked at the Hill Top Diner, where the employees ate breakfast and lunch, so he decided to start his search for JAF there. He drove up to the diner and spotted two of the Southeast service vans in the lot and went in. The two gas men were sitting together near the end of the counter, where Avery took a seat and ordered a soup-and-sandwich lunch. While waiting for his order he examined the men by catching reflective glances off the wall mirrors. He noticed a nametag on one of the men that read: CLIFF WENDT—ROUTE SUPERVISOR. A dispatcher's route schedule was on the counter next to Cliff, and Avery caught a glimpse of the delivery assignments. He was glad to see the assignment list was in alphabetical order, but the top sheet only went up to the letter D. Avery knew the answer was there for the asking, so he decided to take the direct approach.

Avery waited for a conversational gap and turned to the supervisor asking, "Excuse me, my name is Rick Sylvin, and I'm thinking of buying a place down on Merrygold Lane and I noticed that your company services the propane tanks in that area. Is there a standard deliveryperson assigned to that area or is it assigned by need? The only reason I ask is because I won't be there all the time and I want to make sure the tanks are kept full even though the place may be vacant for weeks at a time. I don't want the pipes to freeze up during the winter."

Cliff looked through his dispatcher list and told Avery, "Let's see, Paula Bishop has that route now, and if you want the tanks capped off every week you'll have to call the SG office and leave specific instructions. That shouldn't be a problem, because we have several seasonal customers on that part of the lake and capping the tanks during the winter is regular and common."

Avery stretched his luck, asking Cliff, "Paula, you say? Is she reliable? I don't want any problems, and I'd feel a lot better knowing someone who knows that area was on the job."

Cliff smiled at Avery and said, "Look, Art Fix had that route for over ten years before he disappeared, but Paula is just as reliable. You don't have to worry, mister; she'll do the job right."

Avery's lunch came and he thanked Cliff for easing his concerns. He silently gave himself a high five for getting Art Fix's name, even though the initials were AF and so they didn't match. As the two men left, he overheard one of them say, "You wouldn't catch me buying anything out on Merrygold Lane even if I could afford it; there's too many people dying down there for my taste."

The waitress came and filled Avery's coffee cup. He saw from her tag that her name was Cindy and said, "Thank you, Cindy; the lunch is good." He noticed that the end of the counter was empty except for him and asked Cindy, "Tell me, have you worked here long?"

Cindy smiled and said, "Why, yes. My uncle owns the diner, and I've been here for over five years."

Avery took a chance and asked her, "Then you must know most of the guys from the Southeast Gas Company?"

Cindy said, "Yes, I know most of them and have dated several of them at one time or another. Why?"

Avery took a sip of his coffee and said, "Cliff was telling me the strangest story about one of the guys on his route named Art Fick or Fix or something like that. Cliff said he disappeared and I always wondered how people could just pick up and take off like that. Did you know him?"

Cindy looked at Avery with a little frown on her face. She picked up the cleaning cloth she was using and, crossing her arms, replied, "Yes, I know him, and no, it's not like that. Jed would never leave without a trace like that. He has a wonderful wife and two small children. No, he just wouldn't pick up and take off. Something happened to him, something bad, I think."

Avery sensed she resented his assumption about Jed or Art

or whatever his name was. He asked her, "Jed? I thought his name was Art. Maybe we're not talking about the same guy. I'm sorry if I said anything bad about him; I'm just curious—"

Cindy broke in, saying, "Jethro Arthur Fix. Only his closest friends call him Jed; everyone else calls him Art. He is a good husband and father to his kids. He even took a second job working with those creeps down at the underwater salvage company over in Hemlock earning money to take the family on a vacation to Florida this winter." She wiped off the counter a little and added, "I really screwed that one up when I didn't take him serious six years ago when we were dating. Anyway, he's gone now and those creeps from the salvage company are dead. I don't think he's coming back."

Avery didn't say anything. Cindy went back to the other end of the counter and lit up a cigarette, avoiding any more conversation with him. He had the feeling that Cindy knew more than she was telling. It didn't matter, because she had confirmed whom Avery had suspected of being the person who marked the boathouse next door with the yellow plastic ribbon marker. Jed had contributed in the killing of Karen and Desiree. But it didn't tell him why.

Avery had resolved a couple of questions from his "to do" list. He left the diner more determined than ever to continue his search. As he was driving out of the diner he spotted a telephone company crew working nearby. They were using the same yellow plastic ribbon to mark their working area, and he realized how easily one could get his hands on some. Another question answered.

Avery thought about Jed on his way home and knew that he would not be coming back, ever. Avery also had a feeling that if Jed wasn't dead, he wouldn't have enjoyed his Florida vacation much. He mentally calculated the death toll to be seven. *Why?*

When Avery drove up to his house he saw Heather March standing at his back door with a large manila envelope in her hand, and she looked absolutely stunning.

23

Avery invited Heather into the house and commented on how efficient she had been in obtaining the information he needed on the house. He threw the envelope on the kitchen table and was about to make a pot of coffee when Heather said, "I'm sorry, but I can't stay. I have an appointment to show another house on the other side of the lake, and I'm already running late."

She made her way to the door, where Avery followed her. He invited her back when she finished her house showing, promising to keep the coffee hot. He said, "This will give me a chance to look over the papers you brought and we can talk further about the house when you get back."

Heather thought about his offer and replied, "I can't promise, I don't want to rush my client, and besides, I want to check in back at the office to take care of some business, and . . . sure, coffee sounds good. I'll stop by in a couple of hours if you don't mind."

Avery hesitated a minute and then said, "I'll tell you what. When you get back I'll order pizza and we can go over the information together, that is unless you have other plans of course?"

She smiled and said, "Ave, if you're going to make a business arrangement out of this, then I insist on picking up the pizza on my way back. Besides, I really like my pizza with extra-hot Buffalo-style chicken wings. Besides, I can write it off as a business expense."

Avery nodded and said, "It's a deal; see you later." He walked her to the car, and when she drove off he went into the house and headed directly to the envelope on the kitchen table. He hoped the information would give him a hint about who was behind the house that nobody lived in. He opened the envelope and took out the papers. He smiled at Heather's efficiency, because she had highlighted most of the pertinent information with a pink marker. Avery appreciated this effort because it reflected her personality: neat, precise, and very pink indeed. He thought about it for a minute and came to a decision, that she most likely had earned her reputation as the best real estate agent in the area through hard work and dedication to professionalism. He liked her for that as well as for expressing true sincerity and compassion on the day she showed him the house.

Avery sat down at the kitchen table and started examining the papers Heather had delivered. He separated them in two piles. The first pile contained six pages of building documents. The other pile was made up of four pages of financial information. He started with the building documents, which offered nothing about the builders. He discarded anything that did not contain a business name or individual. He did the same thing with the other pile. When he finished he was left with five pages of information he hoped would provide him with a name he could make a connection with.

Shortly after reading the information, Avery got suspicious and bells started going off in his head. He got the distinct impression someone had intentionally planted a paper trail that was leading nowhere. Avery was sure he had found something that would help him, but he needed an expert.

All the official information was there, including a search and survey. There were legal transactions that named the Walney Manufacturing Company of Jamestown, New York; a subsidiary of Holmquist Industries, Washington, D.C.; and a division of Clark and Associates of Chicago, Illinois. Avery scanned the documents knowing that it would be difficult to determine who actually owned the property. He decided to wait for Heather to return and see if she could shed some light on this mess, because Avery was beginning to see a conspiracy everywhere he looked.

The other papers contained a lot of legal mumbo jumbo with a bunch of disclaimers and lawyer crap, but they also contained signatures. The signatures didn't help him much because they were so difficult to make out they would make the worst doctors' scribbling look like a Dick and Jane book. Avery noticed the legal papers came from the Arbitor, Venquist, and Lansing law firm. He decided that if nothing panned out he would start with them. However, he knew from years of researching for his books that this information was a paper trail designed to give the impression of legitimacy without revealing anything concrete or substantial. Nothing stuck out.

He was rereading some of the papers he had discarded earlier that had no names on them when he heard a car pull in the driveway and saw that it was Heather. He noticed that the pot of coffee was gone and remembered his promise to keep it warm. As Avery busied himself making a fresh pot of coffee, he looked out the window and deduced that Heather must have gone home before returning, because she was wearing jeans and a Buffalo Bills hooded jacket.

Avery opened the door for Heather, and when she came in she set the pizza and wings on the table. Avery absorbed the tangy aroma of the wings. The pizza was hot and smelled good.

Heather looked at Avery, smiling, and said, "I hope you don't mind. I stopped at the office to take care of some last-minute business and ordered the goodies from there. I picked them up after going home to change. I really look forward to getting out of work clothes and into something more relaxing." She walked over to the cupboard and got plates out and started setting the table. Avery was starting to feel like a stranger in his own house and got some sodas out of the refrigerator. As he watched Heather, he gradually realized what was different about her. She was wearing very little makeup and looked a little older, and it suited her.

Avery picked up the papers from the table and said, "No, I don't mind at all. As a matter of fact, I was so engrossed in reading I totally lost track of time and don't even remember turning lights on."

They both sat down at the table, and Heather asked him, "Well, did you find the information you were looking for? Is everything in order?"

Avery broke off a piece of pizza and stuffed a chicken wing in his mouth. After taking a bite, he said, "Pretty much so, but I was wondering who signed the bank closing. I can't read any of the signatures, and I would like to have a name for reference."

Heather picked up the documents and started glancing through them. She held the bank closing sheet up to the light and after studying it for a moment reached in her purse and retrieved a pair of glasses and put them on. After examining the paper more closely, she said, "There is only one person's name on the closing for the purchasers and one from the legal firm. Let's see; Lesley Venquist signed for the legal firm. I recognize her signature from other legal papers in our office. The other is Frederick or possibly Franklin Crawley representing the buyers. Does that help any?" Heather helped herself to the goodies and abruptly added, "Oh, before I forget, there wasn't anything in the file about the construction company, but my father told me that the house was built by an out-of-state company. I understand many of the locals didn't appreciate it much because it took jobs away from the area builders and it sure didn't look good for the Walney Manufacturing Company. Dad did remember that the name on the construction crew trucks was Holmquist."

Avery tried not to seem too surprised about this bit of information but thought it quite interesting, because he secretly knew that Walney, Holmquist, and Clark were one and the same. He picked up the bank closing document and examined the signature of the person representing the buyers. He came to the conclusion that it was Franklin Crawley. Avery stored that name away for future reference but remembered seeing that name earlier when he was going through the other papers. He decided he would look more closely at the papers after Heather was gone. He silently wondered what role Crawley played in the list of companies, industries, and associates.

Avery turned his attention back to Heather, who was studying him intently as he examined the papers, and said, "I'm sorry; I didn't mean to drift off like that. Your father is probably right, because I think it's kind of strange myself that a construction company from Washington, D.C., would be brought all the way to southwest New York to build a house when there are so many good builders in the area."

Heather smiled and said, "You would think so, but I understand that the same company was building another house farther east near the New York–Pennsylvania border and one in the upstate area also. It might have been a contract agreement." Heather realized she still had her glasses on and removed them nonchalantly and put them back in her purse.

Avery didn't want Heather to attach any importance to his interest in the construction company, so he said, "It's not that important and I think I have enough information about the house. Besides, the house is well built regardless of who built it." He was satisfied with getting a name to start with and changed the conversation by asking Heather about her family and how she got into the real estate business.

Heather told Avery that she had lived in the area all her life. Her mother was a retired teacher, and her father had retired early from the railroad. She had graduated from college with a degree in business and was married for a short time to a guy named Tom. She said Tom was a dreamer who failed at everything he tried. Tom went out west in search of his fortune, leaving her several thousand dollars in debt. Heather told Avery that she hadn't heard from her husband in over three years and she was in the process of getting a divorce. She also told Avery that she had gotten herself out of debt and was planning on investing in a lakeside condominium project. Construction was expected to start the next spring.

The evening ended clumsily, because Avery felt that Heather was looking for something he was not able to offer at this time. He was relieved when she accepted his unspoken communications and left with both their dignity intact. When Heather drove off and was out of sight he went back to the papers he had been reading before she came with the goodies. He was halfway through one of the papers when a familiar name popped out at him: Franklin Crawley. It seemed that Mr.

Crawley was somehow associated with the construction order as a representative with Clark and Associates as well as Holmquist Industries. Avery felt quite self-assured that he had found the link he was looking for. He also knew that anyone who would go to great lengths to protect his anonymity would also have safeguards to protect it.

Avery thought about this for a moment and remembered the vision of the skeletal remains of his boathouse and the plastic body bags. He remembered the barbed-wire fence at the house where nobody lived, with private security and frosted windows. He understood that the people he was about to track down were capable of getting the FBI to falsify reports and God knew what else. There were two men dead from the underwater salvage company and one missing. Avery considered all of these things and knew that he would have to be very careful or he could be made to disappear, and there was nobody left in his life who would ask questions if something happened to him.

Avery had turned out the lights and was heading to his bedroom when he had the overwhelming feeling that someone was watching him. He spun around and could have sworn he saw something out the front window, a flash of movement maybe, but when he looked, there was nothing there. His heart was racing and his senses were piqued. He stood there for a long time straining to spot anything out of the ordinary. After a while his self-defense mechanisms returned to normal, and after convincing himself there was nothing there he felt very tired and lonely and suddenly missed Karen. He went into the bedroom and realized his senses were still piqued because even after all this time, he could still smell Karen's perfume and all the other scents that had made her what she was. The house was suddenly full of all the things he had loved her for.

Avery went to the bedroom closet and retrieved his father's .357 Magnum. He loaded it, then spent the night sitting in the rocker. He had more time to think and wondered if his actions, even as careful and planned as they were, had attracted the attention of the people he was after. He didn't know who they were yet, but he had no doubt whatsoever that they knew who he was. This thought made him feel very vulnerable. He decided to call Corry Phillips the next day and get some help tracking down Mr. Franklin Crawley.

24

Jeff Culpepper and his wife arrived at the Lakeside Hotel in time for the first snow of the season and were planning on getting in some early skiing. The indefinite paid leave of absence had been handed down by Franklin Crawley shortly after the meeting. Jeff had learned that Crawley had made the recommendation for indefinite leave to the federal prosecutors' office and it met with little objection. Jeff knew from years of service that this was a precursor to dismissal. He had retained an attorney and filed for a fair hearing, but it would not take place for at least six months, so Jeff decided to spend the time off by doing some investigating on his own. His trip to the lake was intended to dig up evidence that Crawley had a connection in the incident at Merrygold and the deaths at Goldylock's. Jeff also intended on checking out Avery Profrock, who was doing some investigation into the death of his wife. All indications were that this Avery fellow didn't buy the accidental-death certificate issued by Bill Trusk.

Jeff still maintained some unofficial status at the agency, in addition to links with some loyal staff members who would probably be replaced when it was learned that they were helping him. He used this temporary status, and the staff, to run a check on Mr. Profrock. Jeff learned that there were, literally, skeletons in Profrock's closet, that Avery's father had spent a two-year period of enterprising freelance vigilante work in and around the New York City area. The vigilante work ended abruptly when he died of cancer, except for the disappearance of the child rapist/murderer. Through his investigation of Avery Profrock Sr., Jeff concluded that his eldest son, Avery, had taken care of unfinished business and then abandoned his father's work when the old man died. Jeff had believed that the two had rid society of eight or nine of New York's worst until he decided to check out some of the Avery Profrock books his wife was so fond of reading. He discovered that Profrock was using his vigilante experiences as a base for his mystery novels. Jeff suspected that the number of missing dregs might be as high as thirteen and maybe more, based on the amount of books already published. Jeff knew that accessing the CIA file on Profrock would raise some eyebrows at the agency, but if Jeff was departing involuntarily it really didn't matter. Besides, he had learned that the case was purposely held back until the statute of limitations ran out and the CIA had seriously considered recruiting Profrock. After serious consideration Jeff couldn't decide whether to yank the carpet out from under Profrock or let him charge into the lions' den. Knowing what had happened to his wife and niece, Jeff wanted to see what Profrock would do.

Jeff and his wife had been at the hotel less than an hour, and he was making arrangements to look at the Merrygold house through the real estate agent. Jeff didn't really care about the house; he only wanted an excuse to meet Avery Profrock, who lived nearby. Jeff wanted to get close to the man and see for himself if Avery was capable of facing the challenge ahead of him. Jeff also thought he'd treat his wife to an autographed copy of Avery's latest novel.

Jeff dropped Winnie off at the local shopping mall. He checked with the local police to see what progress was being made in the investigation of the two murdered salvage company workers, knowing nothing new would be reported. He did learn, however, that another part-time employee of the salvage company had been reported missing and foul play was suspected.

Jeff picked up Winnie from the mall and went out for lunch before meeting the real estate agent at Merrygold Lane.

They arrived at the Merrygold house at the same time as Heather and parked next to her agency car. Jeff introduced Winnie and himself, and they spent the next half hour or so looking at the house. Jeff knew from the furnishings left at the house that anyone with an ounce of common sense would know that this was not just a meeting place for manufacturing executives and engineers, but a residence for a family with children. He remembered the scene at Goldylock's house and how the Flanigan family had met their deaths. He thought of the 200 spent nine-millimeter shell casings, littering every room of the house.

After Heather had finished showing the Culpeppers the house, Jeff made a reference to the accident that had happened in the fall and feigned concern for future safety. Heather assured them that it was a freak accident and informed them that Mr. Avery Profrock, who had lost his wife and niece in the accident, still lived next door and had shown interest in purchasing the house himself.

Upon hearing this, Jeff looked at his wife and said, "Avery Profrock, isn't that the guy who writes those books you're always reading?"

Winnie replied, "Yes. Would it be possible to meet him? I mean if it wouldn't be an inconvenience."

Jeff thought for a moment, then said, "Please don't bother the man after all he's been through. I don't think it would be polite to impose on him."

Heather considered it for a moment, then said, "No, I'm sure he wouldn't mind at all. He's really a remarkable person. I'm sure he would enjoy meeting you, especially a fan and as possible future neighbors. Besides, if he's serious about buying this place, you may be interested in looking at his house."

Heather left the Culpeppers and went to Avery's house, hoping he wouldn't mind meeting the couple. She soon learned that Avery didn't mind at all, and he even invited them all in for coffee.

Winnie was in her glory meeting her favorite mystery novelist and thought what a wonderful experience it was to be here having coffee with him discussing his books. She was enjoying herself immensely and felt good about starting her first vacation with Jeff after more than five years on such a positive note. But when Avery asked Jeff what he did for a living and he replied that he was retired from a defense contract company, she understood that this meeting was no coincidence. She realized that there was a definite purpose in Jeff's being here. Winnie made a point of never interfering in her husband's work, but tonight she would make an exception. He would have some answering to do. She studied her husband during the remainder of the visit with Mr. Profrock and realized that he was sizing up their host. Jeff was making a precise examination of Avery and his environment. Winnie wasn't sure what her husband was looking for, or for what purpose, but she noticed the entire house had the unquestionable touch of a self-assured, sensitive woman. When Winnie looked into Avery's eyes she saw a man who loved and missed his dead wife a great deal. She saw something else in his eyes but didn't want to believe there was evil in this man, even though she had read all of his books.

Before the trio left, Avery signed a copy of his latest book for Winnie. He informed Jeff that his interest in the house was subject to future writing needs and his immediate need was a storage spot for his boat. Jeff told Avery that they didn't own a boat and if they did buy the house, Avery could keep his boat in the boathouse until he made other arrangements. Jeff reached in his jacket and took out a business card. He wrote his home phone number on it, telling Avery to contact him if he changed his mind about the house. Then Jeff told Avery where he and Winnie were staying and said they would be pleased if he would be their guest for dinner while they were in town. Avery said he couldn't promise, but he would call them if he could.

After Heather and the Culpeppers left, Avery looked at the business card Jeff had given him and the alarms went off. The card introduced Jeff as a representative of Holmquist Industries, Inc.

It was starting to snow lightly while Jeff and Winnie drove back to the hotel in silence. Jeff realized that Winnie knew he had ulterior motives for being here and waited for her inquisition.

Before leaving for their dinner reservation Winnie got all the answers for their being here and made Jeff promise that no harm would come to Avery Profrock. Jeff told Winnie that he would do everything possible to protect Mr. Profrock, but it wasn't Avery's safety he was concerned about. He didn't tell Winnie everything he knew about Avery's history and that after their meeting he was confident Mr. Profrock was more than capable of taking care of himself. Jeff also wondered about his own safety, because if Crawley thought for a minute that Jeff was a threat to his enterprises, whatever they were, he and Winnie were expendable. Jeff reflected for a moment on the CIA report on Avery and concluded that they might have lost an opportunity to recruit someone who would have been a top agent.

Jeff didn't sleep well that night but grappled with moral issues associated with his career and profession. He pondered whether or not to let Avery in on everything.

25

Avery phoned Corry Phillips in Los Angeles and asked him to find out all he could about Mr. Franklin Crawley. Avery also asked Corry to dig up anything he could on Holmquist Industries, Inc. He didn't elaborate, letting Corry believe that he needed the information for initial research into a new book. Corry told Avery he would contact a couple of people in Washington who owed him a favor and get back to him as soon as he could.

Avery walked over to the desk in the den and got out his "To Do" list. He attached the business card Jeff had given him to the list with a paper clip. He then went into the kitchen and retrieved the brown paper lunch bag with the remains of the piece of metal from the propane tank. He examined the piece of metal, wondering where it would lead him. He went to the closet and put the metal souvenir in the inside breast pocket of his heavy winter parka.

Avery had gotten up early that morning and gone into Jamestown, where he purchased two sets of motion sensor spotlights. It took him about three hours to install them, and he decided to go outside and check them out to see if they needed adjustments for optimum detection. They worked better than he expected. They took him by surprise when they lit up the entire property as he rounded the back corner of the house, tripping the sensors. He added another feature to the system that would alert him to unwanted intruders by rigging up an old door buzzer to the same electrical line as the sensor lights. He put his ear up to the den window and could hear the nagging little buzzer going off in the bedroom. He was well pleased with his work. He would sleep better tonight knowing that anybody trying to get close to him, real or imagined, without his knowledge would be detected and, he hoped, deterred.

Avery went back into the house and reset the security system. He then made another call to Corry Phillips and asked him to run a check on Mr. Jeff Culpepper. Avery told Corry that Culpepper was considering buying the house that was next to what used to be his boathouse and he wanted to know a little about his future neighbor. Avery let Corry know that Culpepper was associated with Holmquist Industries, Inc., and said that he just wanted to be sure he wasn't being set up in some way. Corry told Avery that he had contacted a friend in Washington and was waiting for him to return his call and give him some information. Avery thanked him for the effort and apologized for the intrusion, but Corry wouldn't hear of it. He told Avery he'd contact him as soon as he knew anything.

Avery hung up and was on his way into the kitchen when he felt the phone cord tug on his foot. He tried to release the pressure, but it was too late. The phone slid off the table, and it took two healthy bounces off the hardwood floor before coming to rest on its side under the dining room table. Avery cursed under his breath, because it was the only phone in the house. He had been planning on putting in another line after the boathouse was destroyed but never got around to it. If this one was out of commission, he was out of luck until he got to the store to replace it. He reached down and picked the receiver up and knew he was in trouble before he put it to his ear. He heard nothing, nothing at all, not even the annoying buzz sound everyone is accustomed to. He grabbed the rest of the phone and set it back on the table, unplugging it and plugging it back in again. He tried the receiver again, but it was still dead and the situation started to get frustrating. He almost slammed the receiver back into its cradle in anger but stopped. He figured he would try to fix it himself. After all, he had just installed a home security system and should be able to fix a phone. However, Avery kept in mind that installing was one thing, and repairing was something else altogether. He had nothing to lose, because he would just replace the unit in the morning and he had nothing particularly important to do but wait for Corry's call. He examined the phone, knowing his ability at repairing mechanical devices like this was equivalent to his ability at building a rocket launcher, but he was determined to give it his best shot anyway. He started by doing what everyone else does, even the telephone repairman: He banged it on the table . . . no buzz. . . . He unplugged it and plugged it back in again . . . no buzz. . . . He turned the phone upside-down and fiddled with the toner, volume, and anything else that was there . . . no buzz. Then he took the big leap and unscrewed the earpiece and looked inside while probing the wires, wondering if he could get a shock by touching the wrong wire . . . no buzz. He screwed the earpiece back on and unscrewed the mouthpiece and looked inside. He turned the receiver toward the light to see better, and the insides fell out. The wires and inner mechanisms just hung there. Avery began to laugh, because he knew he was in deep shit now. When he reached for the mess to put it back where it came from, something fell out and made a small thunk when it hit the floor. He bent down and picked up what at first looked like a small quartz watch battery with a little tail sticking out. He wondered if it was something that had broken off, causing the phone to malfunction. Avery looked back at the mouthpiece and couldn't see where the piece had broken off and decided to screw the piece back on . . . buzzzzzzzzzzz. Avery suddenly felt like an idiot because he had just realized his phone was bugged. He figured that when the phone hit the floor the bug must have jammed inside, causing some sort of short circuit. Why the phone didn't work wasn't the issue now; his phone being bugged was. He unplugged the phone and returned the bug to the mouthpiece and turned off his answering machine. Avery now knew that the people he was going after were well aware of him and had a distinct advantage over him. They would be coming after him now and he needed information fast.

The old modified Jeep CJ7 had been stored in the garage waiting for winter to rear its ugly head. Avery brought the Jeep back to life when he installed the battery, which had been on a trickle charge for the last couple of weeks. He remembered how Karen had laughed when he bought the Jeep and handed it over to Don, his mechanic, challenging him to convert it into a running machine. Don had had the Jeep for two weeks, and when he delivered it they both spent about an hour gawking under the hood at the 396-cubic-inch Chevrolet engine with a large double-pump carburetor. The Jeep was the fastest four-wheel-drive vehicle in the area. Equipped with oversize steel-studded snow tires, it could handle almost any winter weather short of a blizzard, which was common in this area. Don had a reputation for creating unique vehicles that were capable of outstanding performances. Don's work was greatly appreciated by their owners, and Avery was no exception to the rule. Avery never admitted it, but Karen knew that he enjoyed his little Jeep. It was his favorite toy, with an expensive price tag. It was their private little joke, and Avery would tell Karen, "You'll see; one day you will be glad for having the Jeep. You never know when something like that will play an important role in your life." Avery didn't know it then, but the Jeep would be his most valuable asset and help save his life.

He let the Jeep idle while he made a collect call to Corry from Don's Arco station. Avery decided on the way over to tell Corry that his phone was out because of a snowstorm. Avery didn't know how long his phone had been bugged, but he didn't want to expose Corry any more than he already had. He knew that whoever was keeping track of his phone conversations knew Corry was running a check on Crawley and Culpepper for him. Avery felt pretty confident that Corry was safe in California and wanted to keep it that way. Corry told Avery that he had called his connection in Washington, but there was no information yet. Avery told Corry that he would be in and out of his house for the next week or so and that he had disconnected his answering machine. He told Corry that he didn't expect to be talking to anyone except Corry and would be calling him every other day to keep in touch. Before hanging up, Corry suggested that he call Dan Vitch in Baltimore if he needed information in a hurry. Avery had forgotten about Dan, who was an information specialist that had helped Corry's publishing company on several occasions. Dan was a walking encyclopedia of who's who in government and business.

Avery remembered that Dan was a big fan of his books and was on Corry's list of people who received a personally autographed copy of every one of Avery's books before they went into circulation. Avery remembered that Dan had sent a sympathy card with a note telling him if he could do anything for him to give him a call. Remembering that Dan had written his phone number on the card, Avery decided that he would contact Dan as soon as he got home and got the number from the sympathy card. He could have gotten it from Corry, but he didn't want to involve him any more and it could wait.

Avery noticed some of the running lights attached to the Jeep's exterior roll bar weren't working. He had Don check the toggle switches before he left, because the lights really came in handy in areas that didn't have streetlights. There were eight of the searchlights mounted on the roll bar. Avery remembered coming home one night from shopping with Karen when some idiot heading in the opposite direction on the county road had his high-beam lights on. Avery flashed him a couple of times to lower his lights, because they were almost blinding. Karen reached over and hit two of the toggle switches and the other guy not only lowered his highs; he almost lost control of his car and pulled over to the shoulder of the road. Avery was sure the guy was temporarily blinded. He didn't believe Karen was aware of the light's power, and when she saw the reaction of the other driver her eyes got as big as saucers. When she caught Avery's look of surprise at her impulsive action, she covered her mouth and they both started laughing and couldn't stop. By the time they got home they both rushed into the house and challenged each other for the bathroom, because their kidneys were ready to burst. Avery put a couple extra logs in the bedroom fireplace that night, and the sex was sweet and slow. The laughing continued later that night when Karen remembered the groceries had been left in the Jeep and Avery ran outside half-naked to retrieve them.

When Avery pulled into Merrygold Lane and headed toward the house he knew something was wrong because his security lights were on. He drove past the house and kept going around the bend to the next street, where he stopped the Jeep when he was on the other road and out of sight from Merrygold Lane. He shut off the lights and kept the engine running, although it had a noticeable rumble from the twin exhaust pipes attached to the big engine. He walked a short distance to the tree line blocking the view of his house and watched it for a while until he was confident there was nobody inside. He spent a few minutes scanning the yard and neighboring property before deciding to go back and check it out.

Avery turned the Jeep around and drove back to the house keeping an eye open for any movement. He stopped short of his driveway and stepped out of the Jeep and looked around. There was a fresh layer of snow, and he scanned the area for footprints in the snow but didn't detect anything near the back door. He crept around to the side of the house, from where he could hear the makeshift buzzer going off in the bedroom. As he turned the corner of the house he was cautious not to be taken by surprise. When he was sure no one was there, he looked around and spotted tracks in the snow by the dining room window. He carefully examined the prints and concluded that they were deer tracks. Deer were plentiful in the area and often checked the houses and cottages for food left out by the people who enjoyed watching them. Avery felt safer but checked out the rest of the house before putting the Jeep in the garage and going inside. When he was inside he checked for any signs of entry. There were no puddles on the floor from melting snow that would indicate someone was there or any other hints of an intruder. After Avery was absolutely sure the house was safe, he reset the security system and went around the house making sure all the windows were sealed tight and locked. He then relaxed a little and got the paper shopping bag with all the sympathy cards out of the closet and sorted through them until he found the one from Dan Vitch. Avery stuck the card in his parka, then got out his "To Do" list. He checked off all the things he had investigated during the day.

He was pretty sure the guys on the underwater salvage boat out on the lake the night of the explosion were responsible for the killings. Jethro Arthur Fix from the Southeast Gas Company had marked the boathouse with plastic yellow ribbon. All three were dead. Avery also knew that the boathouse next to his had been targeted, but fate had changed those plans. He studied the list for a while and decided he would call the Buffalo office of the FBI and find out whom agent Bill Trusk answered to. Avery hoped that Dan Vitch could fill him in on Jeff Culpepper and Franklin Crawley. He had a gut feeling that Trusk was associated in some way with Culpepper or Crawley but also had a feeling he might be reading Culpepper wrong because of the way Avery felt like he was being sized up the night Culpepper was at the house with Heather and his wife. If he was somehow involved in the deaths of Karen and Desiree, he wouldn't have made a mistake like leaving a business card connecting him with the killers. Avery made a mental note to tread lightly around Culpepper until he was sure of his connection or intentions.

Before hitting the bed for the night, Avery promised himself to do three things the next day: call Dan Vitch and get information on both men, find out whom Bill Trusk answered to, and get a new dog for Dianne and Walt Beyer. Avery still didn't know why, but felt he would be getting close to who real soon, and then the real work would start.

Before falling asleep Avery wondered again how many more people would die. There was someone else involved in all of this, and he would be added to Avery's list.

26

Franklin Crawley had bided his time and taken a lot of crap along the way to get where he was now. He knew he had to take action soon or lose his opportunity. He also knew he had taken a chance meeting with Manny Carlyle and offering to give him what he wanted most: Jerry Flanigan. The South Americans had offered Crawley something he couldn't get working in a dead-end government job, and his needs would never be met unless he made a change.

The opportunity presented itself when he was recruited by one of the cartel people after being overlooked for the promotion he had been eyeing and realized his future was bleak. He still had control of the Witness Protection Program, and getting rid of Culpepper gave him unlimited access to information that he could manipulate. The new situation kept him in good graces with the government and the cartel. He didn't have any regrets about the people who were sacrificed. He, in fact, found his new-found power exciting and adventurous, not to mention the financial advantages. He knew getting rid of Carlyle would be his biggest challenge and was planning his death very carefully, because he didn't trust Manny one bit. Crawley understood that any mistake would cost him his own life. He knew that Culpepper was snooping around down at the lake, but it didn't concern him. He had taken care of him for good. Culpepper would never work for the government again. Frank would soon have the money and power to hire his own people. He knew if he was patient he could have a couple of congressmen and a senator in his corner by next year. The doors would be wide open for any direction he wanted to take from there. He was very pleased at how quickly things were going his way and wondered why he hadn't made this move years ago. Crawley sat in his private booth at Montero's Restaurant enjoying the expensive wine and imported cigar, feeling quite secure. He had no way of knowing that his world would come crashing down on him very soon.

27

Manny sat in the back of Pete's Hoagie House contemplating what one of his men in South America had just told him after returning from a major deal. His man told Manny that Crawley had met with some of the cartel people and was very friendly with them. Crawley was given the royal treatment just like they gave him when he made a distribution deal for the entire Northeast. Word had it that Crawley had cut a deal for himself, and Manny understood why his last visit to the cartel was not as amiable and friendly as previous trips. He also understood why Crawley acted like a big shot the last time they met, and Manny warned him to keep his place and remember who was paying the bills Crawley had been building up recently.

Manny didn't like the idea of eliminating Crawley, because his future growth depended on Crawley's information and protection. But his entire operation would crumble if he didn't get rid of him and convince the South Americans of his power and control. He understood that the cartel people were making a smart business move. He also understood that if he took the initiative and eliminated Crawley, the cartel would continue dealing with him. After all, they had nothing to lose as long as their product was distributed, regardless of who was doing it.

Manny knew that by now everyone in his operation knew Crawley had cut a deal with the cartel. If Manny didn't take care of business and personally get rid of him, his power and authority would be tested from within. He summoned two of his most trusted men, who had helped him get rid of the three guys at the lake and the Flanigan family. He told them to get ready for another trip.

28

When Avery awoke he felt hungover, because he had spent a rest-less night reviewing recent developments. He was wondering how his life had been reduced to searching for those responsible for taking away everything he held dear. He remembered and half-dreamed of his youth and vacationing every summer with his family. His father had taken the family to this same lake for two weeks every summer. They spent the time camping and fishing. Mother Profrock was a born-and-raised city girl and never really took to camping and fishing but enjoyed the two weeks just the same. It was the only time the family did anything as a family without the intrusions her husband's job as a homicide detective created. Avery remembered that the vacations renewed his parents' closeness and it was a time when the stress of his father's job seemed to disappear after the first week. By the second week there was a lot of laughter and it was good. One summer the vacation was cut short when Avery's mother became ill and they had to go back to New York City early. It wasn't long after that when she seemed to just give up. She died the next year. Avery, Carl, and his father went back to the lake one other time after the boys' mother died, but it wasn't the same. Avery Sr. spent a lot of time thinking of his work and apologizing to the boys. He said that someday he would buy a place on the lake and retire there, but that never came to pass.

Avery and Karen went to the lake after he sold his second book. Karen fell in love with the house at first sight, although they were only thinking about buying a place and promising not to get serious. But Avery saw the look in Karen's eyes and knew there would be no compromising. He made an offer on the place and surprised her when the offer was accepted. They had always intended on buying another place in the south of Florida, where they could go in the winter, a place where Avery could continue his writing, but Karen settled in and kept putting it off. Her father's job had made it necessary for her to relocate every three or four years as a child, and now she wanted to have a place to call home and have some permanence in her life. When the studio apartment was built above the boathouse, Avery started doing all his writing there. It became a permanent arrangement, and they both became accustomed to a routine that was comfortable for both of them. But it was all changed now, and he had business to take care of.

After getting himself showered, shaved, and dressed, Avery drove to a pet store in Jamestown. He bought a miniature schnauzer and drove back to Dianne and Walt Beyer's house. Avery knocked on the door, and Dee looked at him with concern on her face and immediately wanted to know what was wrong. She told Avery that he looked thin and wanted to know if he was eating right and taking care of himself. Avery assured her that he was fine and told her to come to the Jeep.

When Dee got to the Jeep and saw the shivering dog inside, she began crying and took the dog into the house. She immediately started treating it like a long-lost friend. Avery explained that he felt responsible for the death of Wolf and had made a promise to himself to replace the dog when the time was right. If she didn't like this dog, she could take it back and pick out any one she wanted. He knew it wouldn't be necessary, because the dog was already attaching itself to her. The dog wasn't in the house five minutes when it squatted on the kitchen floor and Dee immediately named it Puddles. The naming seemed appropriate to Avery.

Dee brought coffee and they spent a few minutes with small talk. Avery sensed Dee was avoiding conversation that would lead to Karen. He decided to avoid the situation by telling her that his phone was out of order and asked if he could use her phone. He told her it was a long-distance call and he would pay for it, but Dee refused payment and told him to use the phone in the den for privacy. Avery thanked her and went into the room, where he made the call to Dan Vitch. He returned about twenty minutes later and thanked her. They spent some more time catching up on what was happening in the neighborhood. Avery did his best to be sociable, but he was afraid he was doing a miserable job of it. He told Dee he had some business to take care of and asked her to say hello to Walt.

When Avery drove off, he spotted Dee and her new dog standing at the back door. Avery waved to her as he left, but his mind was a thousand miles away. His conversation with Dan Vitch had revealed information that made him feel like he was cast in bronze. He realized that his meeting Jeff Culpepper and his wife was not a coincidental encounter and wondered why Culpepper had come to the lake.

Avery headed towards the hotel primed to confront Culpepper. He had to know what role Jeff played in this whole thing and where he stood.

29

Avery left the Jeep's engine running and the heater on high while sitting in the Lakeside Hotel parking lot. It was snowing and the temperature was hovering near zero. He didn't know how long he had sat there thinking about the information Dan Vitch had given him.

When he called Dan he thanked him for the sympathy card and asked him if he was serious about helping him if he needed it. Dan didn't hesitate a second before telling Avery he meant it and was ready to help him any way he could. Avery told him he needed information on a couple of people associated with Holmquist Industries of Washington, then gave him Crawley's and Culpepper's names and as an afterthought asked him if an FBI agent named Bill Trusk had anything to do with either one of them. Dan took the information and told Avery he would be put on hold while he did some computer searching. After a couple of minutes Dan came back on the line and told Avery he was running up against access blocks on all the computer networks and he wanted to make some phone calls. When Dan came back to Avery, he asked him why he wanted the information. Avery told him he wasn't in a position to reveal the reason and if it was going to cause trouble for Dan he should forget it. Dan was silent for a short time, and when he spoke to Avery again his manner seemed to change, as he took on a very serious attitude. He told Avery that Holmquist Industries was actually a blanket, or cover, for a government agency working with the federal prosecutors' office or the FBI. Dan asked Avery if this information helped him any. Avery said it did, but he could use something more specific. Dan told Avery that if he was interested in Jeff Culpepper and

Franklin Crawley, then he should know the connection with Holmquist Industries was directly related to the Federal Witness Protection Agency. He informed Avery that any further checking on his part would result in some sort of backlash, and to be honest, he wasn't willing to be that helpful. He added that he heard from one person he called that there was some sort of screw-up and Culpepper was relieved of duty as district director. It seems that a federal witness and his family were killed while under protection in his district. Dan also told Avery that Franklin Crawley was Culpepper's direct supervisor and no other information would be available without causing serious repercussions. The conversation came to an end when Dan told Avery that agent Bill Trusk was the FBI's liaison to the federal prosecutor's office in Culpepper's district.

Avery wanted to talk with Culpepper very badly, but there were too many things running around in his head. He drove out of the hotel parking lot to a coffee shop, where he needed time to put it together before confronting Culpepper.

Avery took a booth near the back of the coffee shop and placed his "To Do" list in front of him. The information Dan Vitch had given him filled in many blank spaces. Avery was able to draw a mental image of what had happened the night of the explosion and fire. He figured that if someone was being hidden at the house where nobody lived and someone else, desperate or angry enough, wanted that person out of the way and had the power and money to do it, then the puzzle was no longer muddled.

Avery mentally created a movie of the events leading up to and after the explosion from the information he had obtained. It started with him and Carl leaving the boathouse and their clumsy attempt at grabbing the yellow plastic ribbon flapping off the boathouse entry, then spotting the underwater rescue outfit getting ready to set anchor out in the lake. The next event would be the explosion that sounded different and Avery's feeling that something was wrong. Avery mentally placed himself in the house during and directly after the explosion. He tried to imagine the occupants of the house and their reaction to what was happening. He concluded that they would get the hell out of there in a hurry. If they were there protecting someone, they would leave in a hurry and head directly to an alternate site. Avery remembered Captain Highgate's station wagon and his story of being smashed into by a nondescript car that didn't bother stopping. The car left the scene in a hurry with another car in tow.

Avery remembered his arrival at the boathouse and the scene that had awaited him. He recalled waking the next morning to see many people milling around, including the FBI. He figured that whoever had escaped from the house would call Culpepper. Avery knew Culpepper would take action to secure the area and continue protecting whoever was under his wing. He had answers as to why the FBI was involved and why everything was taken care of so fast. He also understood the connection between Trusk and Culpepper. He now knew who answered to whom. Avery figured that whoever had escaped from the house on Merrygold Lane met his death somewhere else, and Culpepper was either responsible for it or set up to take the blame. As far as Avery was concerned, that was irrelevant, because he was after the person who had arranged the explosion, unless Culpepper was that person. Yes, Avery needed to talk to Culpepper and get to the truth.

Avery drank his coffee and looked at his "To Do" list. He realized that he had many answers, but finding out who owned the house would not necessarily let him know who was responsible for the deaths of Karen, Desiree, and Carl. He knew the reason many people died and how it happened, but only Culpepper could give him the name of the person responsible.

Avery went to the coffee shop pay phone and called the Lakeside Hotel and asked for Mr. Jeffery Culpepper. The operator connected him with the room where Culpepper answered the phone. Avery took the direct approach and told Culpepper, "This is Avery Profrock and I want to talk with you about something we both have in common. Can we meet somewhere and talk."

Culpepper listened to the tone in Avery's voice and knew that he had gotten the information he was nosing around for. He told Avery, "Yes, come to the hotel restaurant in fifteen minutes.

I'll be waiting for you."

Avery thought about Culpepper's plan and said, "OK, I'll be there in fifteen minutes."

Avery wasted no time getting to the hotel, because if Culpepper had plans for getting out of town he wanted to be there to delay his departure. When Avery got to the hotel he saw Culpepper's rental car in the lot, and there were no indications that he and his wife were planning a quick exit. Avery waited fifteen minutes and went to the hotel restaurant where he saw Culpepper and his wife sitting in a booth waiting for him. He walked over and sat in a chair at the open end of the table. He reached inside his parka for the paper bag with the piece of metal from the propane tank that Walt Beyer had given him. Avery took the metal chard out of the bag and laid it down on the table in front of Culpepper and said, "This is what's left of my boathouse apartment and, for all intents and purposes, my life. You have information I need that will make sense of it all. I don't think you're responsible for the deaths of my wife, brother, and niece, but you know who is. It's time to talk."

Avery looked directly into Culpepper's eyes and then to his wife, Winnie. Avery noticed she was staring at her husband with an astonished expression on her face.

Culpepper looked at Avery and then to Winnie. When he saw the look on her face he put his hand on hers. Jeff smiled, telling her, "It's OK. You both have a right to know what's going on, and the truth."

Avery let out a silent sigh of relief, because he didn't want to believe that Culpepper was responsible. He somehow knew inside that Jeff was there to help him.

Jeff was silent while he examined the piece of metal from the propane tank; then when he spoke he looked at Avery, saying, "I'm sorry about everything you've been through and for the deaths of your family members. I had nothing to do with what happened that night, but I was in charge of protecting the people at the house next to your boathouse. I had indications that something was going to happen and should have taken more precautions than I did. I had the family separated and placed in an alternative location, but it wasn't enough, because they all ended up being killed later."

Winnie looked at Jeff and asked, "Does this have something to do with your being suspended? What happened at Goldylock's? What in the hell is going on here?" She looked at Avery and told him, "I realized that my husband had ulterior motives for coming here. When I learned he was here to check you out, I told him to leave you alone, but it seems that you both have something to discuss, so I'll leave you alone. Jeff can fill me in later." Winnie got up and left Jeff and Avery to their confessions.

Jeff looked at Avery and, smiling, said, "Please excuse my wife; she thinks you need protection. She made me promise that nothing would happen to you, but I'm more concerned about her safety. You see, I ran a check on your CIA file and learned that you and your father had some fun for a couple of years doing vigilante work. I truly believe you can take care of yourself without my help. However, I'm a threat to the person who set me up to take the blame for the deaths of the people we were protecting and now I'm expendable. I'm not sure that my wife and I are in danger, but if you keep snooping around I can guarantee someone will be coming after you, if they aren't already."

Jeff noticed a surprised look on Avery's face and sat back in the booth, crossing his arms, saying, "Tell me what you know and we'll go from there."

Avery thought about what he had deduced and filled Jeff in on what he knew and what he suspected had happened on the night of the explosion. He told Jeff about his continued investigation, leaving out the part about Walt Beyer and what he knew. Avery also told Jeff about his conversation with a friend in Baltimore and the events leading up to his phone call earlier. When he was finished filling Jeff in on what he knew, he stopped and, after a short silence, said, "I know what happened, and why, but I don't know who. I think I could find out who was behind this whole thing with a little investigation into who died under your protection and backtracking from there. I can tell you that I think someone had a lot to gain from the death of the witness you were protecting. It wouldn't take a genius to understand that the person who set you up might be associated with the person I want. So you and I can sit here playing a what-if game or we can work together. It's up to you. Either way, I'm going after the bastard who killed my wife and niece."

Jeff held up his hand to silence Avery because a waitress was heading over to the table. When she came, Jeff ordered for both of them. As soon as she was gone, he redirected his attention to Avery and asked, "Is there another Profrock novel in this for you?"

Avery felt the anger shoot out in his eyes but cooled off immediately. He said, "Nope, this is personal and I think my writing days are over." He looked at Jeff and asked, "How about you? What are you after? Pissed off over losing your civil-service job?"

Jeff gave Avery a little scowl and said, "Nope. It's personal. The guy I'm after is responsible for the deaths of seven innocent people and maybe hundreds more. He's got to be stopped before he becomes even more powerful. I'm the only one who knows the truth about him, and I can't prove a thing I know."

Avery looked at Jeff and said, "It looks like we both have something in common but don't know where to go from here, and you have me at a disadvantage." Avery looked around the restaurant to see if anybody was taking interest in their conversation. The tables and booths were far enough apart to provide privacy, but if someone wanted to listen in on them he wouldn't have to strain too hard. Avery turned back to Jeff and told him, "My phone is bugged. Is it your doing or do I have to find out who it is on my own?"

Jeff was surprised to hear this information but tried not to show concern. After checking out the restaurant like Avery did, he asked, "How do you know the phone is bugged?"

Avery described the circumstances that had led up to his discovery of the bug and how he had avoided using the phone since then. He noticed Jeff's reaction to his description of the bug and wondered why he would be surprised. Avery figured the agent would have had a lot of experience with these devices in his line of work. He decided to follow up on his observation and asked Jeff, "Why did you act surprised at my description of the bug?"

Jeff said, "No, I didn't plant the bug, and yes, I am familiar with the type you described. The agency uses them for numerous reasons, including monitoring the safe houses. You see, some of the people we protect in our profession often change their minds about testifying and try to contact friends or relatives to help them get out of their scrape. The bug you described is not your average bug. It not only listens in on phone conversations; it picks up everything in the house and in some cases outside of the house. If your phone has one of these babies, then someone is awfully interested in you and wants to keep track of what you're doing and who you're talking to. If you've been talking to the wrong people or asking the wrong questions, then you could be in big trouble. If I was you, I would have to assume that the bug has been there since the FBI entered the scene." Jeff sat silently waiting for Avery's reaction to what he had said.

Avery thought about what Jeff had said and realized that Corry might not be safe in California after all. Avery was about to say something to Jeff when he suddenly remembered Heather. He had used her to get information about who owned the house and worried that he might have put her in danger. He also had to assume that someone was watching him and keeping his boss informed. He regained his senses and asked Jeff, "What's the connection between Bill Trusk and Franklin Crawley?"

The waitress came with their order and filled their coffee cups before tending to other diners. Jeff purposely waited before answering Avery's question, and when he did he said, "Crawley is probably the one tapping your phone and Trusk is most likely the one responsible for gathering and assimilating information for him. Trusk is an honest person and I doubt that he is dirty. I wouldn't be surprised if Crawley has someone watching us now. You can relax, because we are both being watched and Crawley can't feel threatened, because if he was I would know about it. You see, I still have friends in the agency that keep me informed. Besides, you haven't done anything serious enough for him to take action."

Avery couldn't believe what he was hearing and felt himself getting angry. He decided this was as good a time as ever to ask

Jeff the big question and did by asking, "Who is responsible for the deaths of my wife and niece?"

Jeff thought about lying to Avery but decided that he wouldn't get away with it and told him, "I don't think you know what you're getting yourself into. You and your father did away with some pretty despicable characters, but the guy you want is ten times as dangerous as all the others put together. I will tell you that your guy was able to get away with a lot of killings because of Crawley, but I don't think Trusk is involved." Jeff sat and watched Avery digest the information and realized it wasn't enough. He would have to tell him everything. He waited for Avery's next move.

Avery listened to Jeff and tried to picture the events that led up to the explosion and fire, and agent Trusk's arrival and cover-up of the real causes. He wondered if Jeff was telling him the truth. There was something Jeff said earlier that had grabbed Avery's attention and set off alert bells. He knew it would bother him if he didn't get clarification, so he asked Jeff, "You said earlier that you were worried about something happening at the Merrygold Lane house and you took precautions, but it wasn't enough. What was going on that caused you to feel that something was going to happen and take precautions? Don't tell me it was coincidence, because personally, I don't think you believe in it."

Jeff told Avery about how he had taken precautions at Merrygold because Crawley was taking far too much interest in Flanigan's movements and whereabouts, adding that he thought this interest was uncharacteristic of Crawley. Jeff continued telling Avery that he unofficially had questioned Crawley's motivations in keeping track of Flanigan, because he was an administrator. Crawley had little field experience in the Witness Protection Program, especially those being protected prior to testifying in a trial. He let Avery absorb this information and said, "I know now that Crawley was supplying information to your man and eventually made it possible for him to kill the Flanigan family. Flanigan was going to testify against one of the most powerful drug distributors in the Northeast. Crawley didn't actually kill anyone, but he's just as guilty as if he did. While doing it he was able to make it look like I was responsible. I have small bits of evidence to show that Crawley was behind it, but there's nobody to show it to."

Avery felt uneasy again and asked Jeff, "If you knew Crawley was starting to stink up the agency, why didn't you take more precautions to protect Flanigan and his family?"

Jeff was starting to feel comfortable with Profrock, because he paid attention to detail. He answered, "I knew Crawley didn't know the location of the safe house where the Flanigan family was being held. He got into my secure computer files and found its location the day before the killings. I didn't discover his actions until weeks later, by mistake. I still don't know how he got into my computer files, but by now he knows the location of all the safe houses in the country. If that information is for sale or trade, it's worth millions to the right people."

As Avery listened to Jeff, everything he said sank in. Avery felt sorry for him in a clumsy, weird way, but he was determined to find out who was ultimately responsible and said, "Tell me who was getting the information from Crawley and let me worry about dealing with him. I know you're trying to protect me and keep me from taking chances, but as long as these guys are free, nobody is safe, and you know that more than I do. Besides, I have everything to gain and nothing to lose."

Jeff studied Avery quizzically and said, "I know what you have to lose, but what could you possibly have to gain if I give you the name?"

Jeff didn't know what answer he was looking for but felt he had to find out what made this Profrock fellow tick.

Avery answered immediately saying, "If I go after this guy and lose, I'm dead. And I'll die if I don't. I couldn't go on living knowing that the person who is responsible for what happened, and what continues to happen, is allowed to go free. If I don't get him first, he'll kill me, one way or another."

Avery was waiting for Jeff to respond to what he said and noticed him looking over Avery's shoulder and beyond. He had a welcoming smile on his face.

When Avery turned to see what got Jeff's attention he spotted Heather heading toward their table. When she reached it, she greeted them both, smiling, and said, "I hope I'm not interrupting anything important; you both look so serious. I saw Avery's Jeep outside and decided to stop in and tell him that I spoke to Mr. Dewitt at the boat storage depot. He told me that Ave could keep his boat there for the remainder of the winter, because he wouldn't feel right charging him after what happened. I tried calling a couple of times, but there was no answer and your answering machine isn't working. Is everything OK? You look like you've been arguing. I hope it's not over the house, because I have others just as nice." She giggled and said, "I'm only kidding of course."

Jeff continued smiling at Heather and said, "No, we haven't been arguing. We were just talking sports and got carried away a little. Mr. Profrock has graciously ceded, and Winnie and I are going to be contacting you soon to make an offer."

Heather accepted this information eagerly, saying, "Wonderful! I have the strangest feeling that you two and Avery will become great neighbors and friends." She reached in her purse and wrote her home phone number on the back of one of her business cards, then gave it to Jeff, saying, "I have to meet someone and should be going. Please feel free to call me at home if you feel the urge to make an offer." She was on her way out and suddenly turned back and said to Avery, "I'm hungry for pizza and wings again. If I recall, it's your turn to buy."

Jeff and Avery both watched her as she left, and when she was out the door Avery turned back to Jeff and saw him studying him intensely. There was a moment of silence before Jeff said, "I think you're selling yourself short thinking you have nothing to live for. I've been doing some checking around, and everywhere I go people talk about you like you're their favorite son or brother. After what I just saw in Heather, I think if something happened to you there would be a lot of people who would miss you, and you're right—you have to be protected from yourself."

Avery reached across the table and retrieved the piece of metal left from the propane tank and stuck it back in the pocket of his parka. He folded his hands in front of his chin and said, "I'm not going to say you're wrong, because I have strong feelings for a lot of people around here and would like to keep it that way. But you don't seem to understand my resolve in this matter. If you don't want to help me, then I'll just have to start looking into your business a little deeper and find the information myself. I'm dead serious about this and won't rest until justice is served."

Avery had gotten up and started to leave money for the meal, when Jeff grabbed his arm and said, "Sit down. I want to tell you a little more about the guy you're going after."

Avery looked down at Jeff and saw something in his eyes that led him to believe that he was giving in and after a while sat back in the chair. He waited for what seemed a long time, before Jeff said, "Manny Carlyle is a very dangerous person who takes a great deal of pleasure in killing people. He does it on a regular basis. Manny has many people on his payroll and keeps them in line by killing anybody who threatens him or is disloyal. He always does his killing with at least two of his best men as backups. As best as I have been able to determine, he has been responsible for at least fifty deaths. Avery, this guy is almost impossible to get close to; he's watched by his people at all times. They make sure he isn't taken by surprise. The DEA has been trying to get to him since he took control of drug distribution throughout the entire northeast with little success. You'll be dead before you get a chance to smell his stink."

Avery acted like he wasn't surprised by the information, because he wasn't. He let the air clear a little and asked, "Where is this Manny Carlyle?"

Jeff tried to read Avery, but he couldn't detect anything that would lead him to think Avery was reconsidering his intentions, as nothing was there. Jeff knew he would have to tell Avery, even though after learning Manny's name he could track him down easily. He didn't hesitate but said, "Erie, Pennsylvania." Jeff took one last stab at trying to change Avery's mind but knew it was a waste of time.

Avery smiled at Jeff and said, "Stop worrying; I'm not stupid. Do you think I plan on rushing out after the guy without a plan? That's Carlyle's style, not mine."

Jeff stared at Avery with a blank look on his face, saying nothing, trying to figure out what he meant, when Avery said, "Look, I know what this guy is capable of doing. I've seen it with my own eyes. I've done some investigating on my own. Everywhere this guy goes he leaves dead people lying around. If someone goes after him in his element they wouldn't stand a chance. So, I'm going to make him come to me."

Jeff squinted in thought and after a while said, "Yes, it might just work, but how do you plan on getting Manny to come to you? He's crazy, but he's not stupid."

Avery said, "If everything you've told me about Carlyle is correct, and I have no reason to doubt you, then getting him to come to me is easy. I'll bait him."

The more time Jeff spent with Avery, the more he liked him. Jeff was beginning to understand why Avery's books were so popular. He lit a cigarette and examined it before saying, "It sounds good, but just what do you plan on using for bait? You hardly know anything about the man and you somehow think he will come running."

Avery smiled and said, "Oh, he'll come all right. I'm sure of that. If there's one thing I am sure of, it's that Carlyle is crazy. Despite popular belief, crazy people are very predictable. You know as well as I do that if you threaten or piss off a crazy person, one of two things will happen. They'll either run away, or they'll come after you, and I don't think Carlyle is the running type."

Jeff thought about how Carlyle went after Flanigan until he got him because he was seriously threatened by Flanigan and very pissed off. He couldn't argue with Avery's thinking, but there seemed to be one thing missing, and so he asked him, "What do you plan on using as bait? You don't have anything this guy wants."

Avery's smile seemed to get wider as he said, "There's two things I can use as bait, but it depends on something you told me earlier. You said that the bug I found in my house was the same type used in the safe houses to monitor phone conversations. Did the house where the Flanigan family was killed have one of these bugs?"

Jeff responded immediately: "Yes." He had forgotten about the bugs and silently wondered if they were working that night.

Avery asked him, "Was everything tape-recorded?"

Jeff, beginning to follow where Avery was heading, said, "Yes, all the bugs are taped and kept on file at the central records office. I see where you are heading and yes, the killings would be on the tape unless Crawley had them erased or destroyed."

Avery held up his hand this time to stop Jeff and asked, "Did Crawley know the houses were bugged?"

Jeff became confused again and was losing Avery. He said, "I don't think so. Like I said, he's an administrator and a bureaucrat with little field experience. I doubt he would know about the bugs. As a matter of fact, I forgot about them until you asked."

Jeff remembered the computer printout he had gotten of the telephone calls made from his office the night before the Flanigan family was killed. One of the calls was to the phone booth outside Pete's Hoagie House in Erie. The other was to Goldylock's House. Jeff realized that if the tape was intact it would hold evidence that would prove Crawley had called Goldylock's and link him to the killings. Jeff told Avery about the phone calls made from his office the same night his secure computer files were tampered with. If Crawley was the one who made the calls, and Jeff was very confident of that, he could be confronted with the information.

Avery's smile faded a little when he heard what Jeff said. He stared off in thought for a minute, then said, "I thought so. Crawley is the bait that will bring the polecat out of his hole."

If Jeff could have seen the grin on his face he would probably have been irritated. He said, "Yes, yes indeed. If I can get my hands on those tapes we'll have him."

Avery looked at Jeff and said, "What do you mean *we?*"

Jeff said, "You'll never get the tapes without me. I have a lot of stake here, too. Besides, what else do you have for bait without Crawley?"

Avery wasn't smiling when he looked at Jeff and said, "You.

But I guess you're right, and I don't think you would be cooperative bait. How long would it take you to get the tapes?"

Jeff got up and started walking toward the phone and said, "I'll let you know in a couple minutes."

Avery was eating his toasted BLT when Jeff came back and said, "I'll have the tapes tomorrow afternoon. One of the agency people is putting her job on the line to get them. She said she should have them here tomorrow if they still exist. If they contain the information we need, what do you have in mind?"

Avery said, "First we get the tapes and find out what's on them, then go from there." He fell silent in thought for what seemed a long time, then finally said, "Call your agency friend back and see if she can get the tapes from both houses. We might find something on them that will implicate Manny, too."

Jeff thought about what Avery had said and discovered he was able to keep up with his train of thought and actually look ahead. He knew that Avery was planning on using incriminating evidence to get Crawley to meet with him, then convincing Franklin to contact Carlyle and getting both men together somewhere that would be to his advantage. Jeff wondered if Avery understood what a dangerous scenario he was creating by bringing Crawley, Manny, and most likely two or three of Manny's best men together. He didn't know for sure if Avery had it figured out yet himself. Something was bothering Jeff, and he said, "Look, I don't know what you plan on doing when you get Crawley and Carlyle together, but I think you should know that if you plan something that is going to place innocent people in danger I'll put a stop to you without a second thought about it. Too many people have died because of these guys already. I don't want to be part of anything that will harm anybody but them."

Avery could tell that Jeff was dead serious in his little speech and agreed with him 100 percent. Avery tried his best to soften his posture, even though he was beginning to feel himself getting wound up like he got when he and his father were making plans to rid society of one of their worst. He waited for the air to thin out a little and said, "Nobody is more aware of the death toll because of these guys than me. I don't know exactly what's going to happen when, and if, I get these two guys together. But I will tell you one thing; I won't make complicated plans, because it's too easy to screw up. If things work out right, they'll kill each other and take care of all our problems. Anything that happens between now and then is out of our control. You can be sure that no more innocent people will suffer. If we find a good-enough reason for them to come to us we have the upper hand. All we have to do is pick the meeting place. Anything we plan from there is likely to get us in trouble, so we'd better be sure of what we're going to do."

Jeff relaxed a little bit and nodded in acceptance. He told Avery, "I'll come to your house when the tapes come in, and we can go for a ride in the rental car and listen to them."

They both left the restaurant, and when Avery drove off he wondered how much Jeff would tell Winnie of their plans. He suspected that Winnie would learn just enough to keep her informed but not enough to scare her.

When Avery was about two miles from his house the snow was getting heavier and the wind was creating whiteouts along the North Lake Road. Traffic was near a crawl when he noticed a car off the road facing in the opposite direction. He was concentrating on his driving because the visibility was bad and almost didn't notice that it was Heather's agency car off the road. He checked his rearview mirror to make sure nobody was creeping up behind him. When he saw the road was clear he turned around and went back to Heather's car. When he got close enough to the car he noticed Heather sitting in the car apparently unhurt. He pulled the Jeep off the road and went over to her and noticed she was visibly shaken. He opened the big door and turned off the ignition, telling her to go to the Jeep. After turning on the emergency flashers, he went back to the Jeep and drove her home, where she called a tow truck to retrieve her car.

On the way she told Avery that when she reached in the backseat to get her briefcase she lost control of the car. She turned the steering wheel too hard and went off the road. When

Avery was sure that she was calmed down and under control he told her he would be back in a few hours to take her out for dinner.

Avery drove home and checked out the entire house. When he was sure everything was secure, he showered and dressed for his dinner date with Heather.

30

Jeff went back to his hotel room and told Winnie everything that he and Avery had discussed and planned, leaving out nothing except his knowledge about Profrock's past. She listened intently and didn't interrupt her husband once. After he was finished she asked him one question: "What can I do to help?" Jeff wasn't totally surprised at Winnie's response to his telling her about what he and Avery were planning. Jeff loved his wife a great deal, and had ever since he saw her at the agency when she came in for a job interview fifteen years earlier. His feelings for her never faded. Winnie didn't get the job but ended up taking a job with an advertising company. After ten years she started working three days a week at the office and did the rest of her work at home. She made arrangements to take some leave time so she could come to the lake with Jeff, but her leave was up and he wanted her to go home. She could do nothing to help, and he didn't want her involved. He took her by the hands and said, "Go home, and get back to work. I'll call and let you know if there's anything you can do to help."

Winnie understood that her husband's job could be danger-ous at times and he was capable of dealing with it. She never let on, but she worried for him many times. She always knew when he was working on something that was particularly difficult or threatening because he almost always withdrew and became more focused on his work. She didn't want to distract him or interfere with him while he was working on a difficult case, and she did whatever she could to make it easier for him. She knew that Jeff was serious about his current undertaking. She also knew that when he got like this he was determined. If she was around he would worry about her. She looked at him and said, "Promise?"

Jeff nodded and said, "Promise!"

Winnie went to the hotel room closet and started packing her bag, but Jeff stopped her and said, "Not yet. I'll take you to the airport in the morning."

Jeff and Winnie slept well that night and made love for the first time since he lost his job.

Jeff drove Winnie to the airport early in the morning after a hearty breakfast. Before leaving the airport he called his friend at the agency and learned that she had the tapes. She said she would put them on the next plane out. Jeff had the tapes an hour later. He listened to them on the way back to the lake.

31

Avery stopped at a phone booth on his way to Heather's house and called Corry. He wanted to disassociate himself from Corry and keep him out of harm's way. Avery told Corry that the information he needed was not important and he had gotten what he needed from their friend in Baltimore.

Corry detected something different in Avery's voice but didn't push him. He simply asked him if everything was OK and accepted his assurance with a grain of salt, even though he knew something was being cooked up in his friend's head. He recalled a colleague once referring to Avery as subliminally evil in a Hawthornian way after reading one of his best-sellers. Corry thought about the evil side that Avery kept hidden in a back closet of his mind and felt a chill run through his body. He said his farewell to Avery wishing him luck and telling him to call him if he could do anything.

Before Avery got to Heather's apartment he took his father's pistol out of his parka and stuck it in the little drawer under the driver's side seat and locked it up. He had decided to start carrying it around after meeting with Jeff and getting an earful about Manny Carlyle's likes and dislikes. Avery had a permit for the gun but kept it out of sight just the same because he didn't relish the idea of attracting the type of attention a gun brought. Avery often laughed about how Karen had reacted to the gun, because she always seemed disinterested in it, even though she took great delight in shooting target practice with it and had become quite the marksman. Avery had become accustomed to handguns at an early age and understood very well the power one felt when holding, handling, or firing one. He also knew very well how damaging one like his could be in the hands of someone who knew how to use it. He knew how to use this one better than most.

When Avery got to Heather's place he knocked on her door and waited. He wondered if she was home, because she didn't answer right away. He peeked in the windows along the side of the door and could see her rushing around still hitching her jeans and trying to button them shut. He felt a flush in his cheeks, hoping she hadn't noticed him checking her out. His flush faded quickly when he had a mental glimpse of Karen doing the same thing on several occasions, cursing and threatening never to hang anything in that closet again because everything shrank if left there too long. He decided to be polite and not rush Heather.

When Heather finally came and answered the door he noticed she was not wearing the jeans. She was wearing green wool slacks instead, which seemed to him more comfortable and practical. He knew better than to comment on his observation. He knew from experience with Karen that "comfortable" or "practical" was interpreted as "you must be putting on weight," and he wasn't ready or willing to go through that routine with Heather.

He noticed Heather checking him out; she seemed pleased that he had come dressed casually and said, "I'm glad you didn't get too dressed up, because I ordered pizza and wings and they should be here in about fifteen minutes. I hope you don't mind, but I'm still a little shaken by my experience today and really don't want to go out. By the way, thank you for coming to my rescue this afternoon." She escorted him to the couch, where he noticed a fire in the fireplace that looked inviting and relaxing. Heather put another log on the fire and said, "The car is fine and seems to have come out of the spinout without damage. However, I'll probably be doing some white-knuckle driving for some time to come."

Avery noticed that she was nervous and said to her, "I wouldn't worry about it too much, because something like that can happen to anybody this time of year. As a matter of fact, I get a certain amount of excitement out of experiences like that and feel much more alive afterward."

He couldn't help laughing a little when he noticed Heather looking at him with a sly grin on her face. He asked her what she found humorous, and she said, "Once a boy, always a boy. Why is it that all men seem to get a kick out of things that go bump in the night or cause hair to stand up on their necks? As long as I live I don't think I'll ever understand it. Me, things like that scare the dickens out of me and I need a couple days to calm down."

Avery thought about what she had said and realized she was serious. He asked, "Is there anything I can do to help you?"

Heather turned, facing the fireplace, and said, "I don't want to be alone tonight."

Avery was doing his best not to show his surprise and was searching for the right response to Heather's statement when the pizza deliveryman came, temporarily rescuing him. He went to the door to pay the kid and gave him a generous tip. The kid accepted the tip with a big smile. Before leaving, the kid looked in and when he noticed Heather he gave Avery a wink and a tip of his Yankee baseball cap. Avery stood at the door watching the kid dash off to his delivery truck. Avery couldn't help noticing how much he looked like Carl when he was that age.

Avery walked the pizza and wings to the kitchen and returned to the comfort of the fireplace. He sat down next to Heather and said, "I don't want to be alone tonight either." He reached his arm around to her, and she moved to him, putting her head on his shoulder. Avery could physically feel the tension and stiffness leave her body. She was warm, and she felt good.

They made love in front of the fireplace that night. Later they heated up the pizza and wings in the microwave oven because they had sat a long time and gotten cold, but both ate with a good appetite. After eating they made love again. When a snowplow woke Avery in the middle of the night he watched Heather sleeping and realized he cared for her a great deal. It wasn't love, but it was something binding.

Avery slept better than he had in a long time, and when he woke up he learned that Heather had gone to work. She had left a note on the fireplace mantel that read: "Wow! I dare you to write your impressions of last night in ten words or less without using an adjective. Lock the door when you leave. Call me later."

He smiled, picking up a pen, and wrote: "Is that the warmest you can get your fireplace?" He placed the note back on the mantel and locked the door when he left.

When Avery got to his Jeep he noticed another note under his windshield wiper. He grabbed it and read: "Ave, Winnie has gone home and I need a place to stay. Call me when you're not so busy. Jeff."

Avery studied the note and wondered how Jeff had known where he was, before realizing that if Jeff was heading for his house he would have to pass by the apartment. When he looked, he noticed that his Jeep would have stuck out like a neon light and Jeff would have seen it for sure. He decided to go to the hotel to see what had happened that caused Winnie to go home and why Jeff needed a place to stay.

Avery pulled into the hotel parking lot but didn't see Jeff's rental car. When he started to turn around he spotted Jeff in the lobby looking out at him. He parked the Jeep and went to the lobby, where he learned that Winnie had gone home and he had checked out of the hotel. He was planning on returning the rental car, and Avery offered Karen's Buick as long as he needed it. It had a tape player, unlike his Jeep. He questioned Jeff about his decision to stay at his house.

Jeff told him, "What could it hurt? If they don't know we're aware of the bug, it could work to our advantage. It could also work to our advantage even if they suspect we do know. Think about it."

Avery thought about the possibilities that Jeff spoke of but didn't totally agree that it would work to their advantage. He decided to go along with Jeff's plan anyway, because he found himself wanting to trust him. He asked Jeff, "If you're going to be staying at my house, how are you going to get the tapes when they come in?"

Jeff smiled at Avery and said, "I picked them up this morning when I took Winnie to the airport. I called my agency friend from the airport, and she got the tapes last night. She put them on the first plane out. I hope she doesn't fall asleep at work after starting her day so early. They arrived about an hour after Winnie's plane left, and I listened to them on the way back to the hotel before checking out. You'll be interested in them. I was going to your house when I noticed the Jeep at the apartment house. I didn't want to disturb you. Like I said, you have a lot of people around here that care about you. I left the note on your windshield and came back here to wait for you."

Avery grabbed Jeff's suitcase and started toward the front door, then stopped and asked, "Why did Winnie go home? Was it something you said? I know it's none of my business and you don't have to answer, but I'd feel better knowing she went home under good circumstances."

Jeff grabbed his other bag and followed Avery to the door and said, "She left at my request after I told her everything about what we're planning, leaving out your shady past. Besides, she had to get back to work. In case you've forgotten, I'm unemployed and there's bills to pay. She understands what I'm doing, and why. For what it's worth, she thinks you're a hero."

Avery stopped walking and turned to Jeff and said, "If you need some money to see you over for a while just ask. I had insurance companies tripping over each other recently giving me all kinds of money. The funny thing about it is that I don't really need it. If I can help, just give the word."

Jeff hung his head and shrugged, because he never had anyone willing to help him without strings attached, especially a white man. He put the suitcase down and placed both hands on Avery's shoulders and said, "Thank you for the offer and believe me, I appreciate it more than you could possibly know, but it's not necessary." When Jeff withdrew his hands from Avery's shoulders he was surprised at how muscular he was.

As they drove to Avery's house, Jeff remembered his being recruited for the agency before his discharge from the army. His experience as a security officer and director of special protection of visiting dignitaries gave him the valuable field experience needed for the Witness Protection Program. He had a difficult decision to make, because he wanted to make a career of the military, but he finally decided to accept a position with one of the agency departments specializing in protecting federal witnesses. His work record and success resulted in promotions that were often ridiculed and questioned because many people believed he rose in the ranks due to new minority-hiring mandates. As a result, Jeff found himself working without peer support or respect. He found friends in the agency and arranged for them to work in his department when he was promoted to regional director. These friends were still working with him, even though he no longer had official status. He would never forget their loyalty. His work had been demanding, requiring his constant attention, and it didn't leave him much time for making friends outside of the agency. This new friendship developing between him and Avery was a refreshing experience. He couldn't but wonder what other surprises Avery had in store for him, and as they arrived at the house he was reminded of their reason for coming together. He got out of the Jeep and started preparing himself for the task at hand.

Avery helped Jeff get settled into the spare bedroom. After showing him where everything was, Avery suggested going for a ride in Karen's Buick. He said, "I hope it starts; it's been sitting for a long time."

Jeff walked ahead of Avery and, when he got to the Buick, reached for the door handle and began to open it, but Avery immediately stopped him. He put his finger to his lips in a way to signal Jeff to be silent and closed the door softly. He motioned for Jeff to follow him. Avery opened the side door of the garage and started walking toward the lake. Jeff followed him wondering what in the world he was up to.

When they were far enough away from the house and Avery was sure that the bug couldn't pick up their conversation, he told Jeff, "The doors of the Buick are always locked. I also noticed a greasy palm print on the driver's side quarter panel that shouldn't be there. I saw what looks like scraps of electrician tape underneath the car. I don't know about you, but I'm not sure I want to look under the car to see what might be there."

Jeff didn't look back at the house but instead pointed out at the lake and said, "Pretend you're showing me something."

Avery followed his cue and pointed out at the lake, too, and when he did Jeff said, "I'm going to go back in the house and I want you to go for a short ride in the Jeep. I'll be watching you when you leave to see if anyone follows you."

Avery turned, looking at Dee and Walt's house, and said, "Sounds good to me. We'd better do whatever we're going to do before the neighbors wonder if we've gone crazy out here, pointing out at the lake like this. I'll take a short drive to the convenience store down the road and be back in about twenty minutes. Will that be enough time to check things out?"

Jeff put his hand down and said, "Yes. While you're gone I'll take a look under the car and see what's there."

Avery went directly to the Jeep. He waited for Jeff to get in the house and position himself to see if anyone followed him.

Jeff positioned himself in the doorway between the small living room and Avery's bedroom. From that position Jeff could see out the side windows for any movement when Avery drove off. He spotted the Jeep leaving the driveway. Avery drove up Merrygold Lane, and by the time he reached the main road Jeff had spotted a gray-green Ford sedan easing up the road on the other side of the cove. He recognized it immediately as an agency car. It wasn't one of his but most likely a FBI tail. He felt relieved. Jeff had his problems with the FBI but was fairly certain that they didn't go around putting bombs under civilians' cars. If he hadn't recognized the car following the Jeep as an agency car he would have been very concerned.

Jeff went back to the garage and knelt down, looking under the Buick ever so carefully. He spotted the nasty little package taped under the car near the transmission housing. Jeff had had a lot of explosives training in the army and recognized the unmistakable plastic wrapping around the C-4 explosive, but the wiring didn't look familiar. He crawled under the car as far as he could and realized that whoever had planted the explosive wanted to make sure it worked. It not only was hooked up to the ignition; it had a backup wire with a heat sensor that would work when the transmission got to a certain temperature. If Jeff wasn't so concerned about who planted the device he might have taken a few more minutes to admire the work, but instead he disconnected it and yanked it out. He thoroughly examined the car for other devices, because whoever had taken the precautions in planting this one might have taken the time to connect a secondary explosive. He found nothing. He was wondering what to do with the deadly concoction and decided to hold onto it, thinking it might come in handy later, if he got lucky.

Jeff went back into the house and waited for Avery to return. He wondered how long he had spent defusing the bomb. He didn't have to wait long before he spotted the Jeep coming back to the house. He kept an eye open, and shortly after Avery drove up to the house he again spotted the agency car passing by Merrygold Lane. It passed by and continued on the main road. He only got a glimpse of the driver but recognized him as one of Trusk's men. Jeff wasn't concerned, because Jeff would have the tail called off as soon as he talked with Crawley.

Jeff put the C-4 explosive and the wires in separate paper bags. When Avery came into the house he handed them to him and said, "Take these out to the Jeep and put them in a safe place, but don't put them near the heater."

Avery looked at him with a confused expression and when he looked in the bag, seeing what was there, said, "You're a very handy person to have around. I might keep you." He went to the Jeep and put the bags in the lockbox next to his pistol. When he got back he found Jeff disconnecting the bug.

He watched Jeff as he took the bug to the bathroom and flushed it down the drain. He came back and said, "I know who's been listening to you now, and we don't have to worry about them anymore. After I talk to Crawley they won't be bothering us any longer."

32

Jeff drove the Buick while they listened to the tapes. Avery was surprised at the clarity of the sound produced by the tapes, considering the size of the bugging device used to capture conversations and background noises. He knew incredible technological advancements had been made in the electronics industry since the space program put a man on the moon but never realized how well they had perfected things like this. If he didn't know better, he would think he was sitting in the same room listening to people talking.

Jeff put the first tape in the Buick's sound system, and when it started playing he fast-forwarded it to the day before the explosion. The tape revealed that the agency men at the Merrygold House were talking between themselves about having bad vibrations and that there was something in the air. Jeff forwarded the tape a little more, and Avery paid attention to the phone conversation between one of the men and Franklin Crawley. When the conversation ended, Jeff played it again and heard the phone ringing. The phone was picked up and someone said, "Hello. Who is it?"

The voice on the other end said, "Merrygold, this is Franklin Crawley. Do you recognize who I am?"

The other man responded, "Yes, sir, I certainly do. What can I do for you, sir?"

Crawley responded, "Nothing really. I'm just running an informal security check. How many men on duty, including yourself?"

"One including me. We're on visual and automatic alert and have instituted a code spinoff situation."

Crawley was silent for a few seconds and then said, "Good; maintain present status until further notice." Avery could hear the phone being hung up and wondered what in the hell the conversation meant. He asked Jeff that exact question.

Jeff pulled the Buick to the side of the road and said, "I told you that Crawley didn't have any field experience and that conversation shows me just how little he knew. If Crawley understood what a code spinoff situation meant, your wife and niece would be alive today. You see, a spinoff indicates that there is danger or imminent danger and that the family had been split up and placed in two or more safe houses for ultimate protection. If Crawley knew that, he wouldn't have given Carlyle the information, because Crawley couldn't possibly have known who was being stashed at what house. My men wouldn't divulge that information under a spinoff situation to anybody, except me."

Avery let what Jeff had told him digest for a while and finally said, "You're not telling me everything you know about that night. I don't know how I know that, but if there is more I think you'd better tell me now."

Jeff steered the Buick back on the road and said, "You heard my man on the tape say that they were on visual and automatic alert. Well, that means that one of the men was visually checking out the exterior of the house at all times while the electronic security system, including ground sensors, was in full operation. Merrygold House is equipped with the sensor system because of the close proximity of other houses in the area. The other houses are in isolated areas, and an outside man is always on duty." Jeff stopped for a minute, then turned to Avery and said, "I did some checking after the incident and found out that the entire security system at Merrygold was shut down for a twenty-four-hour period shortly after Crawley made his call. When I checked with the contracted security company, their records show that the shutdown was ordered by me, but *I* didn't give the order. If the system was on line, the men at the house would have been alerted to the presence of someone in the boathouse or anywhere else on the property."

Avery remembered his bull-in-the-china-shop routine the

night he first checked out the house and how the security company had come to investigate his stupidity. He also had a mental flashback of the entire interior of the house and the exhaust fan above the propane tanks and wondered if it was still working its little heart out. His mind kept flashing back to everything that had happened, including his dream where he was trying to find Karen in the warehouse. When he relived the part where he jabbed himself in the finger with the thumbtack from the plastic-covered sign above the propane tank he was jolted back to the present. He unconsciously yanked his hand from his parka pocket. He was shaking slightly and realized he was sweating, although it was near zero out.

Jeff kept driving and they were both silent for a long time until Jeff turned the car into the parking lot of a small plaza and parked. Jeff turned to Avery and said, "There's one more thing on this tape I want you to listen to because I think you have to deal with it in your own way." Jeff pushed the PLAY button and got out of the car.

Avery sat in the car alone listening to the tape. Everything seemed normal, as there was small talk between the men in the house. He heard what must have been Flanigan's voice for the first time, and they seemed to be laughing when suddenly there was a loud KATHUMP sound. Avery realized it was the explosion that had destroyed his boathouse and his life. He listened more and heard the men in the house cursing and yelling. There didn't seem to be panic in their voices, but Avery detected an air of urgency in their conversation as they were leaving the house. He listened carefully and could barely make out the sounds of two cars starting up and their doors slamming shut. Before the tape went silent he could hear the cars leaving the house and what sounded like a crashing sound. He realized what had caused the chain-link gates outside the house to be smashed. He also knew how and why Captain Highgate's station wagon got banged up. When the tape started picking up the noises of fire truck sirens and other emergency equipment Avery pushed the STOP button.

Avery sat in the car for a long while wondering why Jeff had wanted him to listen to that part of the tape. He concluded that it was Jeff's way of letting Avery know that he understood his anguish and was with him all the way.

When Jeff returned to the car he had two large Styrofoam cups of coffee. They drank the coffee in silence for a while until Avery said, "When you drive out of the parking lot take a right and another at the first signal. I think I know a good spot where we can set up a meeting with Crawley."

Jeff started the car and followed Avery's directions. While he drove, Jeff took another tape out of his pocket and stuck it in the player and said, "The Merrygold tape isn't enough to threaten Crawley, but this tape from Goldylock's is something he can't ignore." He forwarded the tape until he got to the part he wanted and they both listened.

Avery heard the phone ringing on the tape and someone answer, saying, "Hello. Who is it?"

"This is Franklin Crawley. I'm calling to make a security check and give you some news. It seems that Director Culpepper has been implicated in the Merrygold incident and is being relieved of duty effective tomorrow. I am going to be implementing new security procedures. How many men are on duty now?"

The other voice on the phone was silent for a long time, and when the man finally spoke he said, "Sir, I don't mean to be disrespectful, but I have no way of confirming your authority, nor can I recognize your security procedures." He was silent again and after a short time said, "I repeat, I cannot recognize or confirm your authority."

Crawley responded, "Yes, of course. I am authorizing and confirming the change of authority. The password is *bell tower*. I repeat: *bell tower*. Do you understand?"

The voice on the other end of the phone responded immediately, "Yes, sir, I understand and recognize. What are your orders, sir?"

Jeff stopped the tape and said to Avery, "I still don't know how Crawley got into my computer files, but he now has the location and passwords of all safe houses in the district. He also has the locations of safe houses in the federal program. My man at

Goldylock's had no alternative but to follow orders from Crawley, because the password was the final fail-safe device and whoever gave it was in control. When you listen to the next part of the tape you will understand just how dangerous Crawley has become."

Jeff restarted the tape and Avery heard Crawley tell the man, "I am instituting a new security plan that will take effect in the morning. I have assigned three new people to relieve your team. Nobody, I repeat, nobody will leave your location or use the phone until the new team arrives. When the new team arrives the password will be *Niagara;* do you understand?"

The man at the house repeated and confirmed Crawley's new orders and recognized the new password. When he was finished he asked, "Is there anything else, sir?"

Crawley responded, "No. Relax. You men have done an excellent job. When you're relieved in the morning you and your men are on a director-authorized vacation; enjoy it."

Jeff shut off the tape again and said, "Beautiful, just beautiful. For all intents and purposes Crawley sealed the team and the entire Flanigan family in the house with no way of confirming the security changes. Then he takes them off guard by telling them they will be going on vacation. When Manny's men show up in the morning with the new password they will be totally off guard and easy to take by surprise."

Jeff reached over and forwarded the tape some more, and when it started to play again Avery listened to the automatic-weapon fire and the shouting and screaming. The tape was silent after a while, only revealing motion noises in the house.

Then someone spoke, saying, "OK, we're done here, Manny; let's get out while the getting is good."

Then another voice said, "Not yet. I want to leave my calling card."

The other voice said, "What for, Manny? They're already dead."

There was the sound of someone walking around and then, BANG...BANG...BANG, more silence, and then BANG...BANG...BANG. Then Avery heard footsteps and

109

someone laughing, the door closing, and then another BANG outside. There was nothing but total silence from there on.

Jeff shut off the tape and said, "I couldn't quite figure out what happened out at Goldylock's until I heard the tape. It all makes sense now.

"When Manny and his men got to the house Manny must have stayed outside with the sentry while the other two went inside. I figure when the shooting started Manny shot the sentry, and then he waited until it was over. Then Manny went inside and left his calling card. Avery, this guy is crazy; he likes to shoot people with a .45 under the chin and through the head. He still did it to the three guards and the entire Flanigan family even though they were already dead."

Avery wondered if Manny was the one who shot the two underwater salvage people that were found in the car trunk. He also wondered if Jed Fix's body would be found someday with the same kind of gunshot to the head. Avery was dwelling on the thought of Manny actually being that near when Jeff broke his chain of thought by asking, "Where are we going anyway?"

Avery came back to reality and said, "There's an expressway up ahead. Take the east ramp and follow the expressway to the Chautauqua Gorge State Park exit."

Jeff followed Avery's directions and when he approached the state park exit he noticed a sign informing travelers that the park was closed for the season. When he took the exit he had to steer hard to the right to follow the ramp under the expressway and Avery said, "Pull over here."

Jeff stopped the car and looked around. He liked what he saw. There was limited traffic because the park was closed, and the spot couldn't be seen easily from the road. It was an ideal spot to meet Crawley. Jeff looked around a little more and asked, "What's up ahead?"

Avery said, "The entrance to the Gorge Park. The road is kept plowed during the winter because maintenance crews come in a couple times a week to check the park buildings and make sure the power sources are working." He pointed to a bridge and told Jeff to drive up the road past the bridge and stop.

Jeff drove up the entrance road, and when he got to the bridge he pulled over and they got out of the car. They walked over to the bridge, and when Jeff looked over the edge he took a step backward, gasping. He told Avery, "I think I ought to let you know that me and high places don't mix well."

The bridge spanned a ravine that was only about 100 feet across, but the drop from the bridge was at least 150 feet, straight down. There was a narrow creek at the bottom. Avery told Jeff, "This used to be a railroad bridge but was converted to vehicular traffic when it became a state park. I understand that the bridge will undergo some renovations next spring because of the low railing."

Jeff stepped up to the railing and agreed with the decision to raise it, because it was only four feet high. The railing was wide and looked sturdy, with those big rivets holding it together, but it was too low. He turned to Avery and said, "I appreciate the history lesson, but I would rather be back in the car and out of here."

They walked back to the car, and Avery stood there for a while checking out the rest of the area. Then he got in the car and told Jeff to drive up the entrance road a little farther. Jeff noticed that the road took another sharp turn to the left about fifty yards past the bridge and there were park entrance gates farther up the road. He told Jeff to stop the car and back up until the bridge behind them came into view from the rear window. He got out of the car and looked around. This spot couldn't be seen from the expressway because a hill blocked the view. He completely scanned the area for any movement.

Jeff wondered what he was doing and asked, "What are you looking for?"

Avery didn't answer him and just kept looking around. After a while Avery looked at Jeff and said, "If Manny and his men can be led to this spot and run off the road, we could pick them off like ducks in a pond." He noticed that Jeff didn't respond to what he said and got back in the car.

Jeff reflected on what Avery had said and decided he didn't want to get in a position where they would have to shoot it out with Manny, unless it was absolutely necessary. Turning to Avery, Jeff said, "First, we have to contact Crawley and convince him that meeting with us is in his best interest." That said, he started the car and headed back to the house, thinking all the way about what to say to Crawley.

As they drove back to the house they were both silent. Avery thought about the Gorge Park and made mental images about the surroundings. He liked the way the park access road allowed for limited access and provided cover for anyone already in the park. It also offered the ability to view the entrance without being detected. The access road curved and straightened out again until it passed over the ravine. Once over the bridge it curved back again until it ended at the park's entrance gate, which was closed and locked. The distance between the expressway exit ramp and the park gate was about one-third of a mile. He estimated that the distance from the expressway underpass to the end of the bridge was about one hundred yards. He particularly liked the way the road turned sharply between the bridge and the gate. Avery believed that if a confrontation with Manny Carlyle was going to take place, he would feel confident of having the advantage here.

33

Franklin Crawley didn't spend much time in his new penthouse apartment because he was too busy contacting people he wanted on his new team. He was sitting at his private booth at Montero's Restaurant with a congressman he knew to be more interested in the financial rewards of his position than his constituents. Franklin had completed a deal with the congressman earlier in the day to support Franklin's appointment to a new agency being attached to the federal drug task force. He made a very sizable contribution to the congressman's war chest. The congressman indicated that he was interested in meeting Franklin's friends in South America and plans were being made to jet the congressman out the next time he met with them when a waiter came to the table and told Franklin he had a phone call.

Franklin excused himself and asked that a phone be brought to the table, knowing it must be important if someone was calling him at the restaurant. When the phone was brought to the table he picked up the receiver and said, "Hello, this is Franklin Crawley. Whom am I speaking to?"

"Franklin, this is Culpepper. I'm sorry to disturb you and I hope you don't mind my getting your whereabouts from the office, but I must speak to you about something very important."

"Culpepper? Listen, I have nothing to talk to you about and if you interfere with me on official business one more time I—"

Franklin suddenly broke off what he was saying and listened to his own voice on the phone. He realized he was hearing a tape recording and didn't like what he was hearing.

Jeff let the tape recording of Franklin's conversation with Goldylock's House play until he got to the part revealing the password and stopped the recorder. He said, "There's more, Crawley." Jeff forwarded the tape to the part where Manny and his men entered the house and killed everyone and then restarted the tape for Crawley to listen.

Crawley listened to the tape recording of the shooting of the Flanigan family and the protection team. He heard the silence afterward and the single shots that were Manny's calling card. As he listened, he became very flushed and got a sick feeling in his stomach.

The congressman was watching him on the phone and when he saw how Crawley was reacting to the phone call he said, "Is something wrong, Frank? You look like someone who just ate a bad clam or something."

Crawley ignored the congressman, listening to the tape until its end. When the tape stopped, Crawley waited for Culpepper to say something, but the line was silent. He finally said, "Where did you get that tape? What are you looking for? Talk to me now, Culpepper, or I will have you picked up and put away."

Jeff waited until Culpepper finished his threats. When Jeff thought his silence was having its ultimate effect he said, "There's several copies of this tape ready to mail out if anything happens to me or any of my family, so listen real close. First, I want you to call off the tail you have on me and Profrock. When I'm sure there's nobody tailing us I'll call you back, but before I hang up tell me if there's any more surprises set for Profrock like the one I found under his car?"

Crawley, fuming, said, "Where in the hell did you get that tape, Culpepper? Who the hell do you think you a—"

Jeff broke in, saying, "Look, Crawley, you only heard one tape and there's more and other evidence that links you with Carlyle and the murders at Goldylock's, so you'd better listen to what I say real close or you'll be the one picked up and put away where nobody will find you." The line was silent for a long time, until Jeff said, "I'm not bluffing, Crawley. Talk to me now or I hang up and make a call to Washington."

Crawley was thinking so fast his head was spinning and he finally said, "OK, OK, what do you want?"

Jeff silently sighed to himself and said, "Get the tail off of us now and tell me there's no more bombs targeted for Profrock."

Crawley said, "OK, I'll call off the tail and don't worry about the surprises. I just learned about it myself and ordered a stop to it already. You have to believe me that I had nothing to do with that surprise and it was done without my authority. What else do you want, and how do I get the tapes?"

"I want whoever is tailing us to call me and tell me he got your order to back off. When that's done I'll call you tomorrow for further instructions."

Crawley agreed and when Jeff started to talk again the phone went dead.

Avery sat listening to Jeff on the phone with Crawley and wondered why he was worried about Crawley taking the threat seriously or not. Avery liked the way Jeff handled himself but wished he had used this opportunity to set up a meeting.

When Jeff hung up the phone, Avery asked, "Why are you waiting until tomorrow to set up the meeting? If you're planning something I'm not included in on, you'd better let me know now."

Jeff smiled as he went to the kitchen for a beer and said, "Look, do you want Carlyle or don't you? If I don't give Crawley time to call Carlyle, the whole thing could get screwed up."

Avery got out of the chair and followed Jeff to the kitchen and said, "How do you figure?"

Jeff sat at one of the kitchen chairs and said, "Crawley is probably on the phone with Manny right now telling him he's in a big bag of shit. He's informing him that we have a tape of both of them that will directly link them to the murders at Goldylock's House. You want Carlyle and I want Crawley. We have to get them both here at the same time or we'll be looking over our shoulder for a long time. Keep in mind that Carlyle is crazy. He won't hesitate killing anybody that causes him a pain in the ass, and he won't give a shit if we have tapes or color videos of him killing someone."

Jeff took a long drink of his beer and waited for Avery to figure it out, but he didn't think Avery followed him. He was about to tell Avery when he said, "I guess you figure on getting Crawley here hoping Carlyle will know what we have planned and take us all out at the same time."

Jeff held up the beer bottle in a salute and said, "Bingo. I'm counting on it. Carlyle can't be in two places at one time. If he wants to cover all the bases, he has to narrow down the playing field."

Avery was silent while he paced the floor thinking about Jeff's plan. After a while he said, "Something is bothering me about your plan, but I can't put my finger on it. What did Crawley say about the bomb under the car?"

Jeff told Avery what Crawley had said and that they didn't have to worry about it anymore.

Avery was uneasy because whenever someone told him not to worry about something it became a priority. He looked at Jeff and said, "If Crawley didn't order the bomb planted under the car, who did? Is this something that Carlyle might do?"

Jeff thought about Avery's question and said, "No, it's not his style."

Avery shook his head and continued pacing the floor. After a long time, he said, "There's got to be someone else involved."

Jeff gave Avery's statement some thought but didn't respond to it. He got up from the kitchen chair and said, "I hope you don't mind, but I was up early and I'm tired. I think I'll go to bed and try to get some sleep."

He was heading to the guest room when Avery said, "I have to ask you a question and I hope you don't take it the wrong way. Why did we drive around in the car listening to the tapes? I mean, after you tossed the bug in the flusher we had no reason to go out. We could have listened to them here."

Jeff paused for a minute. He started walking around the room picking up and examining the things that he believed to have Karen's touch and influence. He picked up a small enameled clay cat that looked like it was made by a small child and set it back down on the desk. He turned to Avery and said, "No, not here. I think there has been enough suffering here already."

With that said he headed to the guest room and he heard Avery say, "Thanks."

Avery was wondering if this would be a good time to hit the sack himself, but the statement he had made about someone else being involved troubled him. He knew he wouldn't sleep well. He sat in silence for a while remembering the day's events when he recalled Heather's note that said: "Call me." He smiled and walked over to the phone and dialed her number. He let the phone ring about five times and was ready to hang up when Heather answered in a groggy voice, saying, "I hope it's important."

Avery's smile got wider as he said, "It's nine-thirty at night. What are you doing in bed? Something keep you up last night?"

Heather replied, "I know what time it is, I'm tired, and yes, something kept me awake last night. Why are you asking so many questions?" Heather could hear Avery laughing slightly and after propping herself up in bed said, "I'm glad you recovered nicely. What did you do all day, sleep?"

Avery said, "As a matter of fact, I've been very busy today showing Jeff Culpepper around, and I think I'll go out again."

Heather was silent for a second, then asked, "What direction are you heading?"

Avery was somewhat surprised by her question and thought about getting clarification but changed his mind and said, "Go back to sleep. I'll call you tomorrow."

He waited for her reply, until she sighed and said, "Coward."

Before Avery could dispute her, she hung up. He stood there with the phone in his hand and said to himself, "I guess she can get the fireplace warmer, but not tonight, fella; you have a test run to make."

Avery looked in on Jeff and saw he was fast asleep. He put on his parka and went to the garage and opened the door. He pushed the Jeep out before starting it up, hoping the rumble of the dual exhausts didn't wake Jeff up.

He drove to the main road and was pleased that it was snowing lightly. The Jeep took a little time to warm up. When he felt it was safe he checked the rearview mirror. When Avery didn't see another car in sight he jammed the accelerator to the floor and the Jeep jumped to life. He liked the way the Jeep responded when asked to perform, and it was doing well tonight. When he was confident that the Jeep could handle the slick road he let off the gas and slowed to the legal speed.

Avery headed the Jeep out of town toward the Chautauqua Gorge Park. When he got to the expressway he hit the gas again until he was traveling at a steady sixty miles an hour. The Jeep didn't break traction, and the four-wheel drive was hardly working up a strain. The road wasn't as slick near the park because the snowplows had recently gone by and spread salt. When he approached the park exit ramp he reached over and set the trip odometer to zero so he could check the distance from the ramp to the park entry gates and again stepped on the gas. The Jeep responded well again, and Avery thought for a minute that he was going too fast to make the curve at the end of the bridge, but the Jeep handled it just fine. When he got to the park gates he looked at the odometer and saw that he had traveled three-tenths of a mile. He put the Jeep in reverse and turned around. When he had the Jeep facing the gorge he crept forward until he could see the bridge beyond the edge of the hill on his right. The snowplows hadn't been through today, and he noticed that the snow was plowed on one side only. He figured the trucks lowered their plow blades when they got to the park exit ramp and pushed the snow off to the side as they went to the gates. Avery figured they didn't bother lowering the blades when they left the park because there wasn't any two-way traffic this time of year. He noticed the snow was piling up against the bridge railing. Avery thought that if this continued to the end of winter the snow would eventually cover the gorge-side bridge railing.

Avery got out of the Jeep and looked around again like he had done during the daylight. He noticed that car headlights were shining against the railing up above, but he was sure that nobody driving by could see down below where he was. He waited until an 18-wheeler passed by and noticed that someone driving a rig like that could see below clearly if he was looking. He knew that there was a curve up there and a good driver would be watching the road, not what was happening down below. Avery liked this spot and knew this was the place for a confrontation. He got back in the Jeep and had driven to the exit ramp back to the expressway when a thought came across his mind. If Jeff couldn't get Crawley and Carlyle to this spot, where would they meet? Avery gave it more thought and decided that Jeff would arrange it.

He drove back to the house and put the Jeep away the same way he got it out. When he went in the house he noticed the kitchen light was on. Jeff must have woken up when he was gone and gone back to bed. He wondered if Jeff had noticed his absence.

34

Avery awoke amid a din of noises coming from the kitchen. There were the sounds of pots banging and drawers opening and closing. At one point Avery heard at least three water glasses break and a loud thud that resulted in a tirade of curses from Jeff. He decided to see what was happening before he had to take Jeff to the hospital. When he got out of bed and went to the door, he found Jeff busy at the range cooking something. He noticed that Jeff had a look of deep thought on his face and knew that he was mentally calculating something. Avery went back to the bedroom and got dressed before seeing what Jeff was concocting on the range and in his head.

Jeff took quite a while finding everything he needed to make breakfast. It was the only thing he was comfortable making, because he never woke Winnie when he got up early and learned to cook for himself. He enjoyed the early morning hours because he was a morning person and did his best thinking at that time of day. This worked out well because Winnie was definitely not a morning person. They became comfortable with the arrangement. He was giving his current situation much thought after a good night's sleep and wondered if he could get Crawley without going through with what was being planned. He suddenly ached for Winnie and made a mental note to call her this evening.

When Avery came into the kitchen he said, "There's bacon in the freezer that would go great with those pancakes if you're interested." He opened the freezer and stuck the package in the microwave oven to thaw out. As they were waiting, he got a cup of coffee. After taking a sip he said, "Give me someone who can make a good pot of coffee and I'm happy; give me someone who can make a good cup of coffee and defuse a bomb, and I'm really happy." Avery sat down at the table and after studying Jeff said, "Tell me something, Jeff. You have all the evidence you need to hang Crawley by the short and curly; why are you still going through with this thing? You pointed out what I have or don't have to gain, but I seem to think that you would benefit more by implicating Crawley in the deaths than doing away with him. So what's the story?"

Jeff grabbed his coffee cup, eased into a chair, and said, "I suspect that Crawley has friends in high places, but I don't know how high they go. He's also got support from people wishing to go up in rank. These people are willing to look the other way to get what they want. I don't know who these people are, and if I go to the wrong people with the information I could be in more trouble than I am now. Besides, I've been accused and removed from duty. That will never go away even if I can implicate Crawley, because it's a good-old-boy system that takes care of their own. I personally believe that most government agencies have been infiltrated by people like Crawley. It's a well-known fact within government agencies and they live with it. I can't anymore. What happened to your family, the Flanigans, and several other people is a good example of what I'm talking about. One last thing: keep in mind that with all that has happened, the only official investigation has been against me."

Avery couldn't do anything but agree with Jeff and said, "I see what you mean." He drank his coffee and thought how he might feel the same way. Jeff was taking care of unfinished business, and Avery respected him for that. Avery got up from the chair and got the bacon out of the microwave oven and said, "Where do you go from here? I mean, what are your plans once this unfinished business is taken care of?"

Jeff grabbed the bacon and started spreading it on the pan and said, "Not sure. Maybe I'll get a nine-to-five job. Maybe write a book. One thing's for sure: I won't make it as a short-order cook." He laughed and Avery was glad to see he had a sense of humor. Jeff turned the bacon and said, "I like collecting miniature Oriental figurines and have quite a collection of them, worth a small fortune. I might try dealing in them or open an antique shop."

Avery fell silent thinking about what Jeff had said, walked to the back window of the kitchen, and looked out at a house that had been the center of attention not so long ago. It looked forlorn as the snow was piling up around it with drifts forming against the chain-link fence. He wondered why the maintenance company hadn't come to clear it away. Avery didn't dislike the house and actually thought it a good buy for someone who wanted a lakeside home with all the comforts. After all, it was built by a government contractor and Avery was sure no cost was spared in building it. He suddenly made a conscious decision about something and walked back to the kitchen table where Jeff was dishing out the breakfast and asked him, "I don't mean to get personal or anything, but I was wondering if you and Winnie were really interested in the house out back?"

Jeff stared at Avery with a slight frown on his brow and said, "Sure. Who wouldn't be? It's a nice place and the price is way below market value, but we couldn't possibly afford it. Why do you ask?"

Avery said, "Like I said yesterday, I had insurance companies tripping all over themselves giving me money after the explosion and fire. You see, Karen was always concerned about what would happen to her if anything ever happened to me and she had insurance on everything. She also had a life insurance policy on both of us. I figure that with the property damage coverage and double indemnity on Karen's life policy I have received about a million dollars already, with more to come. I'm also the sole beneficiary of my brother's estate."

Jeff continued frowning at Avery and asked, "Your brother? What's the story with him? I didn't even know you had a brother. It wasn't mentioned in your CIA file."

Avery told Jeff what had happened to Carl and how he had killed himself after trying to deal with the devastation. He related his trip to Florida and return.

Jeff listened to his story and wondered if he could have dealt with what Avery had gone through in that two-month period and survived to tell about it as casually as he did. He finished his breakfast, even though he didn't really enjoy it much. He took the dishes to the sink and said, "I was going to take one more try at talking you out of this thing, but after hearing about what you went through, I feel kind of foolish. How the hell did you get through it?"

Avery followed Jeff to the sink, got himself another coffee, and said, "What the hell makes you think I have? I would have wasted away to nothing if it wasn't for my neighbor and his wife. I owe them a lot. No, I won't get over this for a long time. Getting justice is just a start. I'll start being myself when that's done."

Jeff smiled at Avery and said, "You mean there's another Avery Profrock I haven't met yet?"

Avery looked at Jeff in an odd way and said, "The mere fact that you're here now planning what we're planning, and knowing more about me than anybody else, should tell you that I am not who I seem to be. But don't let that fool you. To answer your question, unless you plan on sticking around for a while, you'll never meet the other Avery Profrock."

Jeff looked at Avery quizzically and said, "I don't think I understand a word you said, but I'll take your word for it." He thought for a minute, then asked, "What were you getting at when you were telling me about the money and the house?"

Avery said, "Well, if you and Winnie want that house and you're interested in opening an antique shop or something, I might be interested in going into partnership. I have to invest all that money or the tax man will eat me up. Keep in mind that I have a steady income from my book sales, and I am not what you might call money-wise."

Jeff couldn't believe what he was hearing and said, "Why would you make an offer like that to someone you hardly know? You were considering the possibility of putting me on your hit list not too long ago and now you're trying to adopt me. Are you OK?"

Avery smiled and said, "I guess it does sound odd to you, but when, and if, you ever meet the other Avery Profrock, you'll find out that he likes to take care of his friends and keep them around."

Jeff didn't respond to what Avery said but kept going about his business. He was wondering what Winnie would think of Avery's proposition and how she would react. Jeff decided he would mention it to her when he called her this evening. He was wondering to himself if Avery was serious or trying to sidetrack him. Jeff thought he had Avery figured out, but every time he started feeling comfortable around the guy, he did or said something that set Jeff back. He was about to ask Avery where he went last night in the Jeep when the phone rang. They both looked at each other, and Avery waved him to answer it.

Jeff picked up the phone and someone on the other end said, "I got the message from Mr. Crawley, and you're on your own." He hung up the phone and told Avery, "Crawley called off the dogs; when do you want to arrange the meeting?"

Avery walked over to the coatrack and grabbed his parka, saying, "Later. I have some business to take care of first." Before Jeff could say anything, Avery was out the back door and heading for the garage. Jeff watched Avery drive off in the Jeep. He understood that Avery was going somewhere to do something that Jeff couldn't help him with.

35

Avery drove past Heather's apartment building and continued into town. He had been making a mental list of people he wanted added to his new will since discovering that the explosion and fire were not an accident. His first stop would be at the bank, where he would pay off all his bills and get a total of his assets, and then he would go to his lawyer.

The next stop would be at the cemetery where Karen was buried. Avery hadn't been there since the funeral. He knew it was something he had put off far too long.

When Avery got to the bank he learned that his total worth, including properties, was in excess of $2 million. He paid off what he owed on the boat and mortgage. There was another $160,000 in investments that Karen had toyed with from an original $10,000 start over ten years earlier. The safe-deposit box contained another $20,000 that Avery kept handy for emergencies. He gathered all the documentation of the funds and went to his lawyer's office, where he made out a will that named Walt and Dee Beyer as the recipients of two-thirds of the total amount. He named Corry Phillips as the executor for the remainder to dispose of as he felt fit. The lawyer wondered why Avery hadn't lived better, considering his assets, and told him he should at least buy himself a decent car and get rid of the Jeep. Avery laughed and said, "You're probably right, but there's a lot to be said for blue jeans and old Jeeps."

He signed the new documents and left. Avery had nothing personal against his lawyer and, in fact, found him intelligent, amiable, and sincerely concerned for his clients. Karen took care of all the legal matters, including his contractual agreements with his publishing company. She worked with accountants keeping track of the taxes, and Avery could relate to all of them, but not lawyers. Like his father, Avery felt uncomfortable around lawyers, because he felt they were crooks with a license. He knew most lawyers disliked the way their profession was maligned by the actions of some of their colleagues, but it didn't take away the bad taste left in his mouth when he was around them too long. His father had felt that the worst place in the world to get justice was in the courts, and Avery felt the same way. Even though he stopped vigilante work after his father died, he saw nothing done to change the way things were done in the courts. In fact, he felt the situation was getting worse.

When Avery left the lawyer's office he headed toward the cemetery but stopped at the DuBois Funeral Home and made arrangements for his own funeral and paid in advance before leaving. By the time this was done it was mid-afternoon and he decided to call Heather's office and see if she was interested in having dinner with him. Heather accepted the offer gladly, and they made arrangements to meet at a local steak house after Heather showed a house later in the day.

The cemetery was well kept even though there was a lot of snow, and Avery appreciated that. He drove to the spot where Karen's grave was located and found himself sitting in the Jeep for a long time before he could move. When he finally got out of the Jeep he looked around, trying to remember the day of the funeral, but could only remember bits and pieces. He recalled the limousine ride to the burial site and sitting in a folding chair facing the casket. He remembered familiar faces, sad faces.

He walked heavily toward the grave, and spotting the headstone, he stopped. It was the first time he had seen the headstone with Karen's name, date of birth, and date of death. It was a shattering jolt of reality for Avery, and he felt an overwhelming sense of permanence when viewing the engraved notice. He knew Karen was dead and buried, but until now he never really understood that she was gone. He stared at the marker for a long time and after a while walked closer, where he noticed a lot of footprints in the snow. They were small footprints. Lying at the base of the marker was a small wicker basket with an assortment of flowers in it. There was a card in the basket, and Avery bent down and picked it up and read: "Thank you, Mrs. P., we miss you a lot." The card was signed by twenty-three fourth-grade students from the Northtown Elementary School class where Karen had spent three days a week volunteering, helping children with reading and other skill needs.

Avery looked at the marker again and realized that it was Karen's birthday the previous day. He had a serious guilt trip for not remembering, even though she was no longer around. He remembered the two cards that had come in the mail yesterday addressed to Karen and realized they must be birthday cards from someone who didn't know about the accident—no, not an accident, a killing. He made a mental note to check the cards and contact the people to give them the bad news. As he walked back to the Jeep he made another mental note to thank Dee Beyer for picking out the headstone, because he knew he didn't. As he drove off he promised to come back when his business with Crawley and Carlyle was taken care of, preferably in an upright position. Deep down, Avery knew that Karen would not approve of what he was planning, but he would make his apologies later. First he had to make the world of the living a little safer.

36

Heather sat at the restaurant table in amazement because she had never known anyone with an appetite like Avery. He had eaten a sixteen-ounce Porterhouse, baked potato, salad, garlic bread, and a side order of mushrooms. She joked that if anyone came in and saw them they would think they were waiting for their meal instead of just finishing one, because Avery's plate looked as clean as if it just came out of the dishwasher. When Avery ordered pumpkin-ice-cream pie for dessert she could have sworn she added a whole inch to her thighs. She looked at Avery and said, "There's a lot of evil in the world and I think it's a sin that some people can eat anything and not put on a pound. I didn't eat much tonight, but after watching you I may have to go on a diet."

Avery laughed while he ate the pie and said, "Yes, I agree."

Heather looked at Avery with a surprised expression on her face and asked, "What do you mean, you agree? Do you think I should go on a diet? What are you trying to say?"

Avery realized at once that he had said the wrong thing and put both hands up in a defensive gesture, pleading, "No, no, not at all. What I was agreeing to was your statement about there being a lot of evil in the world. In fact, there's more than you will ever know, and I hope you are never confronted with it." He let Heather calm down a bit, then said, "Trust me on this one." He waited again and said, "The other night when you were asleep I was watching you and I am a little embarrassed to admit it, but I checked you out. You've got the body of one of those Olympic sprinters, long legs and no fat."

Heather flushed a little and asked, "Really? I hope so,

because I take special interest in how I look. Thank you." She smiled and said, "Speaking of evil, do you think your houseguest would mind staying at the house alone tonight?"

Avery smiled back at her and said, "Nope. As a matter of fact, Jeff and I are going in business together." He reached in his sport coat pocket for his checkbook and wrote out a check for $110,000. He handed it to Heather saying, "I believe this is a reasonable offer for the house on Merrygold Lane. See if the owners will accept the check in full payment and have the papers drawn up."

Heather looked at the check and said, "I can guarantee that this offer will be accepted." She put the check in her purse, shaking her head a little. She looked up and said, "It must be nice to be able to write checks that are bank-ensured to the amount of $300,000. What kind of business are you and Jeff going into?"

Avery thought about Heather's question, smiled slyly, and said, "Antiques and maybe some sort of cleaning business." He was studying Heather's reaction and said, "Before you say anything, I think you should know I'm a good judge of character and I know what I'm doing."

Heather dismissed whatever she was thinking of saying and smiled. She thought a minute and said, "I hope you and Jeff are very successful and make lots of money. Is this business proposition the reason you're in such good spirits tonight, or is it something else? You seem a little excited about something. Care to share it with me?"

Avery didn't want to lie to Heather, because Jeff had called Crawley before he left for their dinner date and arranged a meeting. He was excited about meeting with Crawley and decided to tell Heather a half-truth. After giving it some thought, Avery told her about his visit to the cemetery and resolving some unfinished business. He hoped what he said didn't spoil the mood for Heather and felt good when she said, "Oh, Avery, I'm so pleased for you. I can't imagine how difficult it must have been for you."

When the waitress came to fill their coffee they were already gone. Avery and Heather made love that night, and it had a special quality to it, as if it was their last night on earth. Avery knew that it could very possibly be his last night and lay awake most of the night listening to winter sounds outside. He wondered if Jeff was getting any sleep.

37

Jeff had called Crawley before Avery went to dinner with Heather. He had thought about how to arrange the meeting all day while Avery was out taking care of his business, whatever it was.

They both discussed Jeff's plan before calling Crawley and decided to meet him at the same small plaza where Avery had sat in the car listening to the tape of his boathouse exploding. They knew that Crawley would call Carlyle as soon as he learned where they were going to meet. Jeff and Avery knew that the two would try to set up some kind of trap for them, but they had plans of their own. They planned on leading them to the Gorge Park area and seeing what developed. They knew they had to get them out of the populated area and in a spot that gave Jeff and Avery an advantage, and that meant the park.

Crawley tried to convince Jeff to come to him and get this situation resolved. However, Jeff knew he had the advantage and told Crawley, "If you want the tapes in your hands, then you come to me. Keep in mind that I have several copies ready to mail to people who will follow my instructions to the letter."

Crawley said, "What assurance do I have that you won't mail the other tapes?"

Jeff's intentions were to have Crawley write a letter of resignation explaining that Jeff had had nothing to do with the deaths of the Flanigan family. It was the only chance he had of ever getting his job back. He knew the only thing he had to bargain with was the tapes and once Crawley had them he would be expendable. He answered Crawley's question in one word: "None."

Crawley decided he wasn't going to fool around with Jeff anymore because he had called Manny from the restaurant as soon as he got off the phone with him yesterday. Manny had told Crawley not to mess with the guy, because he had the tapes. Crawley had no way of knowing Manny didn't care in the least about the tapes and planned on getting rid of all of them anyway, especially Crawley.

Crawley thought about what Jeff had said and after a silence said, "OK. Where and when do you want to meet?"

Jeff gave Crawley directions to the plaza and told him, "Tomorrow night, park in front of Betty's Beauty Salon at the far end of the plaza. Make sure no other cars are near you. If you get there early, drive around until the plaza closes and make sure you're alone." As an afterthought he asked Crawley, "What kind of car will you be driving?"

Crawley smiled to himself and said, "A gray Mercedes."

Jeff replied, "Manny Carlyle must pay you a lot of money for your information. Be there tomorrow night or the tapes get mailed out." With that said, Jeff hung up.

Jeff and Avery talked about the meeting and decided that when Crawley arrived at the plaza they would lead him to the park. They planned on using two cars. Jeff would keep watch from the coffee shop across the street from the plaza. Avery would come when Jeff called him from Don's gas station. Jeff wanted to be there early in case someone else showed up, so he and Avery could be ready to make a change in plans.

Avery agreed with Jeff's plan to be prepared for change and reluctantly agreed to let Jeff keep watch on the plaza while he waited at Don's place. They both did some brainstorming and made a simple plan to head for the Gorge Park if anything went wrong. When the plan was agreed on by both of them, Avery left for his dinner with Heather.

After Avery was gone, Jeff called Winnie and let her in on what was happening but didn't tell her about the possibility of Manny Carlyle showing up and messing the plans up. Jeff did his best to assure Winnie that he and Avery would be safe. He told her they had taken all necessary precautions, but he wasn't sure whether she bought his story. He let it rest and told her about Avery's offer to go into business with him and that he was considering the offer.

Winnie listened to her husband and did everything she could not to let him know how worried she was for him. She was relieved when Jeff changed the topic. When she heard about what Avery had offered Jeff, she wondered what Avery had, or didn't have, on his mind. She worried that Jeff had hitched his wagon to a psychotic horse.

Jeff didn't want Winnie worrying about things and told her that Avery was a levelheaded person who had gone through more than one person should have to go through. He told her that Avery knew what he was doing, then he asked her to think about Avery's offer and said he would talk to her more about it tomorrow.

Winnie listened to what Jeff was telling her and felt better by the time their conversation ended. She made Jeff promise to call the next day and let her know what she could do to help.

Jeff told her to go to work and have faith that everything would work out for the best. They made arrangements to talk again the next day.

38

Avery was dressed and out of Heather's apartment before her alarm went off. He had been wavering in and out of sleep and decided to leave before his stirring woke her. He knew he would be able to get some sleep in his own bed. When he got home he found Jeff had had the same problem. He was watching an old black-and-white movie on the television. Avery stood in the doorway for a minute trying to remember what the movie was, then gave up. He went to his room without a word to Jeff and could hear him laughing in the other room before dropping off to sleep.

When Avery awoke he could have sworn he only slept ten minutes, but four hours had passed and it was 10:00 A.M. Jeff was still asleep in the other room.

Avery passed the morning checking the mail and contacting the two college friends who had sent the birthday cards, both unaware of Karen's death. They were sorry to hear the news and gave Avery their best. He had never really met any of Karen's friends and after talking with these two regretted never having the opportunity.

Avery went to the supermarket and did some shopping. When he returned, Jeff was at the kitchen table cleaning his service revolver. Avery put the groceries away, then went out to the Jeep and got his revolver, and Jeff cleaned it for him. They avoided conversation about their meeting with Crawley until later in the afternoon, when Avery told Jeff that he was going to Don's service station about seven o'clock. Jeff decided that he would head for the coffee shop around eight. Once there he would call Avery to make sure the phone connection was OK.

They both spent the afternoon trying to relax, but it was an exercise in futility, because all they accomplished was bumping into each other while roaming around the house aimlessly and apologizing.

They spent some time trying to figure out what to make for lunch and after a long while settled for canned soup and cold-cut sandwiches. They both managed a short nap in the afternoon and were well rested before leaving for their vantage points.

39

Manny and his two best men left after dinner at Pete's before the two-hour drive to the lake. Manny was as excited as a kid getting ready for his first Little League baseball game. The prospect of getting rid of the two jerks causing all the trouble out at the lake and Crawley in the same move was a bonus for Manny. He had made a phone call to his new man and given him instructions to be there early and be ready to take out all of them if he had a clear shot. The new guy was a pleasant surprise with great potential. If the new man didn't have to be pulled out on those two jerks at the lake to do some agency work, he would have taken them out long ago. Manny was giving a lot of thought about using government officials in his organization and made a decision to recruit more people like this new guy. There were definite advantages to recruiting lower-level government people, because they seemed more loyal, not like that asshole Crawley, who had his sights set too high from the beginning. Manny laughed a little at the thought of trying to get Crawley to kill someone himself. When Manny told the new guy that he would be given an opportunity to kill Mr. Franklin Crawley from the Witness Protection Program, the guy was so excited he almost pissed his pants. Manny had no doubts whatsoever that he would do the job and not miss if he got a clear shot. Knowing that was very assuring to Manny, because they were going after a couple of guys he knew would be ready for him. Manny wanted to kill Crawley himself, but he needed Crawley as bait to get the other two. It was fine with him, because he liked the way this whole situation was prearranged for him. He was almost ready to leave for his trip to kill Crawley when the idiot called him and told him about the tapes he thought Manny cared about. It would take more than a couple of tapes to cause Manny to sweat, because he could make almost anything disappear with a phone call and the right amount of money.

Manny sat in the back of the big Lincoln Town Car during the drive to the lake while taking care of business from the cellular phone. His position had changed since his ascent to the top. He remembered how hard he had worked for the big bucks, but his new power was worth more to him than the money. He never took drugs because they could never match the high he got from the power and control of being in charge. He was looking forward to the high he would get tonight.

They found the spot where Crawley would be parking and drove around to check out the area before settling into a parking lot about a block away from the spot. Manny had his driver back into the lot facing the plaza so he could have a clear view of the action. Manny liked what he saw and knew his man would have a clear shot at Crawley. Manny also knew Culpepper would have quite a surprise when he showed up. He told his men to keep their eyes open and wake him when the plaza started closing up for the night. Manny was sleeping when Crawley arrived.

40

Franklin Crawley left for the lake after a late lunch with a state senator. The four-hour drive gave Crawley the opportunity to plan his future. He was totally oblivious to the fact that Manny Carlyle had known his every move since returning from his last trip to South America. Crawley liked the way Manny was cool under pressure and told him that he would take care of the two at the lake. When he had called Manny and told him what instructions Culpepper had given him, he sensed a different tone in Manny's voice. He seemed to have an almost brotherly attitude toward Crawley. He didn't like being patronized by Manny, but if it meant getting rid of Culpepper and the tapes he would take it with a grain of salt. Besides, Manny wouldn't be giving anybody orders after tonight.

Before leaving for the lake, Crawley stopped at his apartment and got his service revolver. He hadn't carried it in over a year and a half but hoped to use it tonight to kill Manny.

Franklin started getting nervous because the weather was getting bad and it was snowing harder the closer he got to the lake. He was worried he would get there late and screw everything up. He felt better as the snow stopped when he got closer to the lake. As it turned out, his timing was good, as the plaza parking lot was starting to thin out. He drove around for a while before spotting the beauty salon Culpepper had instructed him to park near. Crawley took the opportunity to stop at a store and buy some pipe tobacco and then went to the plaza, where he parked his car at the end of the lot near the salon. He shut off the engine and packed his pipe in preparation for Culpepper's arrival.

Crawley lit his pipe and was thinking about the price it would cost to have the senator on his team when he heard a noise that reminded him of a crystal glass stem breaking and felt something bounce off his shoulder. He looked down on the seat and saw a piece of glass, and when he looked up he noticed a hole in his windshield about the size of a dime. He moved to get a closer look at the hole and felt a sudden pain in his chest, and when he looked there was a spot of blood. The next shot came just as he was about to ask what the hell was going on and caught him above his left eyebrow. The impact slammed his head back into the headrest, and that's where it stayed, and that's where Crawley died.

The sniper waited for his next target to come into view through his night-vision scope. He had seen Culpepper around before and looked forward to putting the next shot right between his eyes. The other guy, Profrock, would be easy. The assassin remembered the day at the lake when he was helping the cleanup crew at Merrygold House and seeing Profrock pass out when he saw his wife's body being loaded in the coroner's wagon. He laughed then and he had laughed earlier that night, but he would never laugh again.

41

Jeff left the house about an hour after Avery left for Don's place. When Jeff got to the coffee shop he called to let Avery know that he was positioned. He drank coffee while watching the Plaza parking lot. He saw the gray Mercedes drive by once and knew Crawley was waiting for the lot to clear out before parking. He thought to himself, *Good. Everything is going as planned so far.*

While watching the plaza, he also checked around to see if anyone was taking an interest in him or looked out of place, especially Carlyle. Jeff wasn't sure what he was looking for but knew he would be able to tell if something was wrong. He knew Carlyle wouldn't be far away.

The plaza parking lot was almost empty when Jeff saw the Mercedes pass by the coffee shop. It pulled into the lot and parked at the far end near the beauty salon. When he was sure nobody had followed Crawley, he went to the phone and called Avery to let him know he was going to the car.

42

Avery pulled into Don's station and had the tank filled. He could see the plaza from the spot even though it was three blocks away. There were still a lot of cars in the lot. He asked Don if he had a few minutes to look at the Jeep, because he wanted some special work done on it.

Don said, "Sure. What do you have in mind?"

Avery said, "If I asked you to weld some heavy sheet metal to the inside of the Jeep, could you do it now?"

Don looked at Avery quizzically and said, "Ave, if you're looking to add a little weight to this mother all you have to do is put some sandbags in the back, but I don't think you really need it."

Avery smiled at Don and said, "No, not more weight. I'm looking for something that will stop a nine-millimeter slug."

Don looked around to see if anyone had heard what Avery said, then pulled him to the back of the station and asked, "Ave, if you're in some kind of trouble let me know. I'll go over to the bar and grill and get a couple of the Neanderthal types in there. They'll take care of your problem at my asking. I mean, if you're in some kind of trouble where people are coming after you with guns, well, I mean to tell you, you don't want to fuck around with that stuff, my friend."

Avery told Don, "No. Thanks for the offer, but this is something I have to take care of myself. I can take care of anything facing me. What I need is something to protect my backside, if you know what I mean?"

Don squinted at Avery, studying him for a minute, and said, "You know, I've wondered about you. Come to think about it, I bet you can handle yourself in a scrape and I imagine you've been in a couple. OK, what do you have in mind?"

"I need some metal welded to the back gate to protect me from behind. Can you do it?"

Without hesitation, Don drove the Jeep into one of the service bays. In less than five minutes he had the door pins removed and the Jeep's back gate on a workbench and measured.

Avery stayed out of Don's way and watched him work in a way that reminded Avery of a carpenter preparing a piece of wood for a difficult angle cut. Don finished his measurements, noting his observations on a wall calendar depicting half-naked women. Don scooted to the back storage room, and Avery heard him talking to himself and cursing under his breath. After a short time he heard crashing and banging noises. Shortly, Don emerged with two pieces of stainless-steel sheeting about one-eighth of an inch thick. He placed one of the sheets down on the workbench and after fumbling around in a drawer produced an odd-shaped hammer that looked like a mountain climber's pick. Don raised the hammer and rapped the steel sheeting with all his might. Avery jumped back a little, wondering if Don was losing it, and realized that he was testing its durability.

Don tossed the hammer back in the drawer and examined the sheet proclaiming, "Beautiful. I knew this would come in handy someday. I got this stuff out of that little diner that was taken down to make room for the new bridge." He looked at Avery and said, "It will take more than one of those popguns to go through this shit." He placed the sheets up against the Jeep's gate and made the proper markings and started welding them into position. Before welding the top piece, he cut a slit into it and asked Avery, "Is this going to be big enough to see out your rearview mirror? I don't want to make it too big and let a lucky shot get through."

Avery examined the slit and told Don, "Perfect."

With that done, Don finished the welding.

Avery was going to help him hold the gate in position while he put the pins back in place when the kid tending the gas pumps told him, "There's a phone call for you, Mr. Profrock."

Avery went to the phone, and Jeff said, "I'm at the coffee shop and everything looks good from here. How's things there?"

Avery said, "Just fine. I have a good view of the plaza from here. As soon as I see you drive the Buick up to Crawley's car I'll drive up to meet you."

Jeff, feeling better about the plan, said, "Good. I'll call you back before I leave the coffee shop."

Avery hung up and went back to give Don a hand, but when he returned he found the mechanic checking the gate and making sure everything was OK.

Don stepped back to examine and admire his work and after a moment said, "Can't even tell it's there." He walked over to Avery and, taking him by the elbow, led him to his office, where he opened a steel filing cabinet.

Avery followed Don's lead, and when he got to the office he looked around smiling inwardly, because the office was the same as almost all service station offices. When he was young, he and Carl would often go to the station down the street from their house and get cold Coco-Cola from the soda machine out front. Sometimes when work was slow, Mr. Walney would let them sit in the office and he would tell them stories of his youth and how good the kids had it today. Avery remembered Mr. Walney's office was just like Don's. There was an old distributor cap on the desk to hold pencils, piles of bundled rust-colored rags on the floor, a piece of wood with a long nail sticking out of it to hold receipts, a pair of greasy coveralls hanging from a nail on the back of the toilet door, and many other things that let one know that he was in a service station office. But, most of all, there was the perpetual combination of smells like sweat, oil, antifreeze, and transmission fluid. It was an environment that would repulse someone who thought himself refined, but Avery found it comforting in a down-to-earth fashion. It wasn't sophisticated, but it had character and Avery liked places like this, the same way he liked old barns and stony creek beds.

When Don opened the cabinet he reached in the back and got out an old cigar box and walked over to the desk and pushed papers and other junk to the side. He sat down and motioned

Avery to sit in the other chair in the office. Avery did as instructed and when he was seated, Don opened the box. He made sure nobody was watching, then took out a .38 revolver wrapped in one of the rust-colored rags. He unwrapped the rag and examined the gun before loading it and handing it to Avery, saying, "This is not registered and can't be traced. I don't know what kind of trouble you're in and I don't want to know. But I like you and I would kick myself in the ass if something happened to you and I didn't do anything to help. Take it and be careful. It has a hair trigger, so don't shoot yourself in the foot."

Avery knew he was being taken into Don's confidence and didn't want to disillusion him because he believed Don chose his friends carefully. He remembered Don telling him one time after he finished the engine work on the Jeep about being a prisoner of war. Avery seriously doubted anyone else around the lake knew about it. He could feel the weight of the .357 snugly resting in its shoulder harness under his parka. He knew the .38 didn't have the firing power to match his piece but stuck it in his pocket just the same and said, "Look, Don, I don't know how to thank you for everything you've done. I really appreciate this and someday when this is all over we can sit down and I'll tell you all about it."

Don got up from the desk and stuck the cigar box back in the cabinet saying, "Don't thank me; just bring that gun back. When you do I'll tell you the story behind it. Is there anything else I can do for you?"

Avery was intrigued by Don's promise to tell him the story behind the .38 and made a note to take him up on it. He said, "Yes. I need to park the Jeep out in front awhile. Is that OK?"

Don snorted and shook his head and, smiling, said, "No problem, just make sure you don't get in some sort of shoot-out in front. I pay enough insurance on this place already." He went into the outer office, and Avery got three crisp $100 bills out of his wallet and stuck them on the wooden peg with the long spike sticking out of it.

Avery drove the Jeep out to the front of the station and backed it against a snow pile. He settled in for the wait, and it wasn't long before he spotted the big gray Mercedes-Benz driving by slowly. He got his first and last look at Franklin Crawley when he had to stop for someone pulling out of a parking spot along the curb. What he saw reminded him of a television cartoon he liked to watch when he was a kid, *Mr. Magoo*.

Avery waited for the meeting to occur, and the thought of the unknown haunted him and chipped away at his mind. He was not totally comfortable with this plan because there was another unnamed player in this game and he didn't know if, or when, he would show up. He kept this thought in mind, and it helped him stay alert. He gave the kid working the pumps ten dollars and told him to let him know when he got the call from Jeff. After the call came, Avery went back to the Jeep and started it up and waited until he saw Jeff pull up to Crawley's car. Avery had started pulling out of the service station when he noticed something was wrong. He saw Jeff drive up to Crawley's car and walk up to it. Avery realized there was a problem when Jeff started running back to the Buick and took a diving sprawl behind it. Avery slammed the gas pedal to the floor, and before he got to the parking lot he was glad he had the metal sheeting welded to the back gate, because he could hear the slugs making dull thudding noises when they hit from behind. He knew he had to get to Jeff fast, because the shots were coming from behind him and if someone up ahead was ready to open up on him they would be caught in a crossfire.

43

Jeff had waited for what seemed an eternity, but when Crawley arrived and parked his Mercedes where instructed things happened pretty fast. Jeff waited until he was certain Crawley was alone, then called Avery to let him know he was leaving to get Crawley to follow them to the Gorge Park.

In the time it took Jeff to call Avery and get to the Buick Crawley was dead. Jeff drove purposely toward the plaza parking lot, pulling in at a spot where he could approach the Mercedes from behind. He stopped about twenty feet to the side of Crawley and a little to the rear. He tooted the Buick's horn to get Crawley's attention so he could motion him to follow, but Crawley didn't seem to notice him. Jeff laid on the horn again and, when Crawley didn't respond, decided to get out of the car and tell him to follow him.

Jeff got out of the Buick and quickly looked around before approaching Crawley. When all seemed safe he walked over to the Mercedes and suddenly realized something was terribly wrong. He was certain that if Crawley was alert and waiting for him he would have been able to see him approach the Mercedes easily, but he didn't move and when Jeff got closer he realized Crawley was never going to see anything again or write a confession. Jeff took a closer look and noticed the two bullet holes in the windshield. He was wondering what the hell had happened when combat instinct took over. Jeff took a quick look across the street to where the shots that killed Crawley must have come from and noticed a slight movement between two large evergreens. He acted without thinking by running away from view. He ran toward the Buick and when he was near enough dove for cover just in time to feel the familiar sting of a bullet graze by his right ear. He got behind the Buick and another bullet hit the car's bumper and Jeff knew that he was being targeted. Jeff couldn't hear the shots and realized whoever was shooting at him was using a silencer. Another shot bounced off the cement and ripped through his pant cuff, missing skin and bone. Jeff was in big trouble and desperately looked for a way out of his trap. He was considering making a dash for the coffee shop. He estimated he would have about five seconds to find cover again, because the shooter would have him targeted if he took any longer. He was about to make the move when he heard the horn from Avery's Jeep and saw him coming at a high rage of speed. He could see Avery reach over, opening the passenger-side door of the Jeep, heading right toward him. The Jeep came to an abrupt stop and Jeff made a leaping jump inside. He spotted another car coming up on the Jeep's rear as he jumped in. Avery wasted no time getting the Jeep moving out of the danger zone. Jeff tried to tell Avery to look out to his left because there was a shooter in the trees but was too late. A bullet struck the windshield frame just to the left of the steering wheel and Avery hit the gas hard and they were heading out of harm's way.

Avery heard Jeff's warning about the shooter and responded, "I'm more concerned with the shooters behind us. See if you can get a couple rounds at them and try to back them off a little while I put some distance between us."

Jeff rolled down the window and tried to position himself to get off a couple shots at the car following them, but when he looked the car was stopped and he told Avery, "Relax; they stopped. I think we're out of danger."

Avery said, "You can relax if you want; I'm not. If my guess is right, whoever it is stopped to pick up the shooter. Now I know who the someone else is that I was worried about."

Jeff looked back and said, "You're right; they're coming after us again. What do we do now?"

Avery looked at Jeff with a nervous smile and said, "We stick to the plan and head for the Gorge Park. It's the best chance we have. Besides, we know the area and they don't; that gives us a slight edge. If my other guess is right, the people following us are Manny Carlyle and his men. What happened to Crawley?"

Jeff took a peek in the door-mounted rearview mirror and saw the big car following, but unable to get any closer to the Jeep. He turned back to Avery and said, "He's dead. He took two shots and one of them caught him where it counts. Why couldn't I see it coming? Carlyle isn't the type to take threats like we made seriously and would like nothing more than to get rid of all of us. I miscalculated and now we're in big trouble."

Avery reached over and poked Jeff in the arm and said, "Stop it. I knew Carlyle was crazy, but I didn't think that he would make a move like this. He used Crawley to set a trap for us like we were planning for him. I doubt he knows that and he probably thinks he has us on the run like a rabbit. That might be what costs him dearly."

44

Manny sat in the back of the Lincoln whooping it up like he was on a roller-coaster ride. He especially liked it when Crawley took his last breath and Culpepper was on the run. Manny got a ring-side view through his binoculars, and now the chase was on. He had his man stop and pick up the shooter and gave him a "Well done" when he was in the car. Manny reached in his pocket and handed the shooter an envelope with the promised $10,000. The shooter stuck the money in his coat as he reattached the night scope to his other rifle.

Manny told the driver to step on it and catch up with the Jeep, because while it was better equipped to the climate, but it couldn't outrun this Lincoln. He reached in the backseat glove box and took out his nine-millimeter and lowered the power window. He was trying to get off a shot when the Jeep pulled away. His driver said, "That's no ordinary Jeep, boss. It must have a lot of horsepower under the hood."

Manny snapped back at the driver, "I don't want excuses, pussy; step on it and catch up with him."

The driver hit the gas pedal before Manny finished his sentence because he already knew he had crossed him and didn't want to worsen the situation.

The other of Manny's men rolled down his window and aimed his .357 Magnum and pulled the trigger. He knew he hit the Jeep's back gate because the sparks flew on impact. He heard Manny laughing in the backseat and emptied his gun into the Jeep. He was reloading the gun to get off some more shots when the Jeep made a turn onto the expressway. He would have to wait.

The driver had to slow down to make the turn onto the ramp,

because no matter what Manny said, he wasn't going to get in hot water for smashing up before they had a chance to kill these guys. As soon as he reached the straightaway he punched the gas pedal again and started catching up with them. He wished the Jeep would crash and get this thing over with in a hurry.

45

Avery slowed down a little before coming to the expressway ramp so the Lincoln could stay close enough to keep them in sight. Jeff objected because they were being shot at, but he relaxed a little when he noticed the alterations to the back gate of the Jeep and asked, "When did you find time to do that? Nice touch."

Avery smiled again and said, "I had it done while I was at Don's place waiting for Crawley to arrive. It seems to be working well." He no sooner said that when the windshield was blown out by a slug that got through the slit in the metal shield. Avery hit the gas again to put a little more distance between them. Jeff recoiled when the windshield blew out, because the glass was flying everywhere and the onrush of cold air made it difficult to see.

Avery knew they had made two mistakes already and was glad to see that there was little traffic on the expressway because there were no guarantees that they would have a safe drive to the park. He didn't want innocent people getting hurt because of them. The park exit was coming up next and he didn't want to get too far ahead and lose the Lincoln. He looked in his door-mounted mirror and couldn't see them. He worried that they had given up the chase in favor of another day. Then he remembered who was chasing them and knew they wouldn't give up that easily. He wondered if the driver had lost control of the car and left the expressway involuntarily. Avery was considering turning around when another barrage of bullets hit the back of the Jeep; they sounded closer this time. He looked in the mirror again and realized their pursuers had turned off their lights and crept up on them. He again slammed the gas pedal to the floor and the Jeep jolted ahead, and he was able to get far enough ahead to be somewhat safe until he got to the park exit.

46

Manny was getting frustrated with the chase and knew this Profrock guy had balls. He told the driver to turn off the lights and when he did they were able to creep up on them. They were able to get off some good shots, but they seemed to have little effect. Manny said, "There guys must have a bullet-proof shield or something. We put enough shots into that Jeep to send it to the junkyard, but it keeps on going." He told the driver to back off and see where they were heading. "We got the whole night to chase these guys around, and I don't want to have to come back tomorrow to finish the job. There will be government people crawling all over the place when they find Crawley's body, and I don't want to be around."

The driver backed off and turned the headlights back on and followed the Jeep wherever it was heading. They were starting to relax a little when the driver said, "They're getting ready to turn again. It looks like they want to get off the expressway."

Manny moved up in the seat so he could see better and said, "Don't let them get out of your sight, but keep back far enough so he doesn't pull a fast one on us."

They all saw what was left of the Jeep's taillights and noticed it turning into a park entrance and Manny said, "Why would they go there? The park must be closed." He gave it some thought and said, "I don't like it. These guys are smarter than I gave them credit for, and we have to be very careful." He told his driver to slow down. When they were making the sharp turn to the park entrance road Manny told the driver, "Stop here."

The driver stopped and Manny told the shooter, "I want you to get out here and find a good place to get them in your sights.

If they come out of that road before us, put that thing on automatic and let them have it."

The shooter got out of the car and headed for a spot that would give him a clear view of the road leading up to the park entrance.

The rest of the men watched the Jeep go up the road and around a bend. Manny wondered how far the road went into the woods and said, "I don't like this one bit. It looks like a trap to me, and we have to be very careful with these two guys. You guys got any suggestions?"

The driver said, "I don't think it's a trap, boss. I say we go in there as fast as we can. If they have some sort of trap, they'll be taken by surprise if we come in fast with guns shooting."

The other man said, "I agree. I don't think these guys are capable of handling what we can deliver. I say we go in hot and heavy. Besides, this is the only way out and we got the shooter waiting for them."

Manny was thinking about what the other two had in mind. He was considering scrapping the whole thing when the driver said, "Hey, boss, remember the time we took out Tony B. and his two men? If I remember, it was a situation just like this, except in an alley."

Manny started laughing and said, "Yeah, and those guys knew what they were doing. OK, let's go for it."

They all checked their guns and reloaded. When they were all ready they headed in at full speed ready to start firing.

The shooter took a position under the expressway and waited for the action.

47

Avery looked back and noticed that the Lincoln had backed off and its lights were on again. He told Jeff, "I think they've given up the shoot-'em-up stuff for now. They've backed off a little and are keeping their distance. Just in time, because the park entrance is coming up and I want them to get there before they go off the road and kill someone besides themselves."

Jeff looked back for his own confirmation, and when he saw that they were keeping their distance he felt a little relieved and said, "Good. The sooner we're in the park, the better. Now that this thing is developing the way we want, what's next?"

Avery was silent for a minute and then said, "The mistakes are two to none in their favor. I hope they want to get this thing over quick, and make their first mistake."

Jeff looked at Avery and didn't say anything as they entered the park entrance road. He drove slowly enough so Manny and his men could keep track of where they were going. As soon as the Jeep was over the ravine bridge Avery sped up. He waited until the last minute and slammed on the brakes just before the tall gates blocking the entrance. He steered hard at the same time, bringing the Jeep to a stop facing in the opposite direction. He turned off the lights and crept forward until the Lincoln's headlights were in view.

Jeff suddenly realized where Avery had gone with the Jeep the other night and said, "I hope you never fail to amaze me, friend."

They both took out their revolvers and released the safeties and waited for Manny to make the next move. They didn't have to wait long. When the big car started heading toward them they were sure Manny and his men wouldn't see them until it was too late.

48

Manny's driver turned off the headlights again and put the Lincoln's transmission in D-1 for better traction and stepped on the gas. Manny and his other man were leaning far out the side windows with their feet braced against the back of the front seat for support. They were ready to start firing as soon as they saw the Jeep.

It had started snowing again and the wind was creating a steady flow of white powder across the road leading to the park entrance. The Lincoln broke traction every time the rear wheels skidded across a drift. The driver was one of Manny's best and knew enough to keep the pedal to the floor or the big car would never get up enough speed to take their quarry by surprise. The Jeep had better traction and more speed, but the road was only wide enough for one car at a time and all the speed and traction didn't mean squat. The road was like a one-way street now, and the quarry wouldn't be able to get past the Lincoln without meeting head-on.

The big car was building up speed very fast and the driver knew he was in control. Manny, hanging out the window just behind the driver, was hooting and hollering like a wild Mongol yelling for him to go faster, faster, keep it going.

The driver was just about to tell Manny that they were in good shape when something happened and the big car broke traction, causing the rear end to bang up against the frozen snowbank. The snow on the side of the bridge was frozen solid. It caused a slight nudge and the car was beginning to straighten out when something caused the windshield to explode. The driver yelled out in pain when the .357 slug ripped out a large chunk of his right shoulder. The slug went through the driver's shoulder and passed through the seat, where it finally stopped deep in the thigh of Manny's number-two man leaning out the passenger-side window. The number-two man screamed in pain and immediately drew back inside the car, where he crumpled to the rear seat in agony.

Manny had dug his feet deeper under the front seat when the car slid and hit the snowbank. He saw the muzzle flash from a short distance ahead just before the windshield blew out and his driver screamed in pain. Manny immediately let loose with his automatic until the thirty-round clip was empty. He reached in his coat pocket for another clip when the night suddenly became alive with a bright flash of light. The car was out of control.

The driver couldn't feel anything in his right arm and grabbed the steering wheel with his left. He had pulled the wheel to get the car straightened out again when he was suddenly blinded by light. He released his grip on the steering wheel to cover his eyes and lost control of the car.

Manny was trying to figure out what was happening when the Lincoln took a severe jolt. When he tried to look to the spot where the lights were coming from he only saw darkness and a gaping hole in the earth. Manny realized that the car was out of control and everything seemed to be happening in slow motion. He was trying to get back inside the car to grab the steering wheel when the rear of the car hit something hard, causing Manny to be slammed up against the window frame. He felt his right ankle snap and his shoulder shatter. Manny didn't feel the pain until he realized that they were in a hopeless situation. He was able to get back inside the car just as it started its tumble into the gorge. He braced himself as best he could and grabbed hold of the door handle for support. His efforts would be just enough to keep him alive, temporarily.

49

Avery and Jeff waited for Manny to make his move. They hoped to run the Lincoln off the road and get it stuck in the snow, where Manny and his men would be trapped.

Avery showed Jeff how to turn on the overhead running lights and told him to hit all the switches at once when Avery gave the order. Then he told Jeff, "I'm going to drive the Jeep around this curve; I think the hill on our right will keep us partially hidden from their view. I don't know what they have in mind, but I hope they make a move soon, or we'll have to go after them. When they come, hit the toggle switches; maybe we can force them off the road."

Jeff reached down and placed his fingers in the position where he would be able to turn on all the toggle switches at the same time. He wondered what Manny was planning and agreed with Avery but really didn't want to go after Manny because then their edge would be lost.

Jeff turned to Avery and said, "Keep the Jeep as far to the right side of the road as you can. I don't want to get hit head-on by the Lincoln. Nothing personal, but this Jeep is not equipped for that kind of action."

Avery said, "I agree, but we don't want to get stuck either. These things are great for this kind of weather, but if you get stuck in one of these things, you're stuck like you've never been stuck before." He eased the Jeep over to the right side of the road as much as he could, and the Jeep held the line. He was getting closer to the ravine bridge when he spotted the Lincoln heading toward them with its lights off.

They both raised their pistols at the same time and aimed.

Avery could see better from his side of the Jeep and told Jeff, "Uh-oh, here they come, and there's two of them hanging out of the car taking aim." Avery was just about to fire off a couple of shots when the Lincoln lost traction and slid into the snowbank and veered off target a little. He waited to see what the driver was going to do, and when the Lincoln got straightened out again they both took two shots each. One of the shots would find the mark and create an irreversible chain of events.

Shots were returned from the Lincoln almost immediately, but they were wild and off target.

Avery could see the rapid muzzle flash of an automatic weapon and heard bullets bouncing off the front of the Jeep. He thought that if the shooter had held the gun up just a hair higher, he and Jeff both would be dead. The Lincoln veered again and Avery yelled, "Now! Hit the lights now!"

Jeff hit the toggle switches and was surprised at how much light they produced. The Lincoln was flooded with the light, and he could see the driver try to cover his eyes. When the driver took his hand off the wheel the big car went out of control, heading straight for the snowbank and open field.

Jeff and Avery watched what happened next and both would recall how it seemed to unfold in slow motion.

The Lincoln's windshield was gone, and when Jeff turned on the Jeep's running lights they could see the driver trying to cover his eyes from the intense glare. Manny was hanging out of the window just behind the driver, and it looked like he was screaming something at him. The car was out of control as it headed directly toward the snowbank at high speed. When it hit, the Lincoln went into the air like it was leaving a ramp. It hit at an odd angle and lifted into the air. The big car started rolling with its front end pointing toward the sky. A huge spray of frozen snow from the bank flew out in front of the car, and it looked like a shower of diamonds. The car built up momentum and started spinning. Avery and Jeff could see the men inside bouncing around like rag dolls. Avery wasn't sure, but it looked like Manny was trying to get back inside the car.

The car's spin slowed down and it started to fall back to

earth. It passed out of the running lights' range. Avery thought the Lincoln was going to come crashing down on the bridge, and that would be fine with him, but its momentum had carried it out away from the road. The Lincoln came down and the left rear fender smashed on the top of the bridge railing. When the Lincoln hit the railing, the trunk sprang open and all sorts of junk came out, littering the bridge. The car bounced off the railing and did a flip as if catapulted from a trampoline. The car started flipping end over end until it flipped over the railing and out of sight. Avery saw the Lincoln's taillights as it fell into the gorge. The night air became suddenly quiet.

Jeff observed the same thing but from a slightly different angle. When the Lincoln hit the railing and disappeared into the ravine he gasped and said, "Holy shit."

Avery got out of the Jeep as soon as the Lincoln went over the railing, and he could hear faint crashing noises at the bottom of the ravine. When the crashing noises stopped he ran over to the railing and could hear rocks rolling and bouncing off the ravine wall below. He looked down and could see a small fire burning around the crumpled car. Jeff came up beside him and again said, "Holy shit."

Avery looked around and saw nothing happening on the expressway above. The only noise was the distant rumbling of the Jeep's exhaust pipes, which were sending a steady flow of steam rising into the night air. Rocks and stones continued creating echoes down in the ravine. It seemed eerily quiet, and Avery said, "Come on; let's get out of here."

Jeff was looking over the railing and could see the fire spreading and knew the gas tank must have burst and caught fire. He had turned to follow Avery back to the Jeep when he heard a sharp cracking noise off to his left and he squatted down, looking in the direction of the noise. He recognized it as a rifle shot. The gunshot noise reverberated and echoed all around him. He turned to Avery to warn him and saw him standing in the middle of the bridge looking in the same direction with a quizzical expression on his face.

Avery finally realized what was happening and had turned

to run to the Jeep when another shot rang out. Jeff saw Avery get hit with the shot, and it looked like he had been smashed in the chest with a sledgehammer. Avery was thrown backward and slammed to the bridge surface.

Jeff reacted instinctively from his combat experience and started heading toward the Jeep for cover. He knew the next shot would be at him. He took about five running steps and heard the shot that clipped the calf of his left leg as he dove for the Jeep.

Avery was lying on the bridge and his chest felt like a thumb the day after it was whacked a good one with a hammer. He couldn't move from his prone position and he was having trouble breathing. He looked up just in time to see Jeff heading in his direction. Avery saw a muzzle flash coming from just under the expressway overpass and heard the shot that got Jeff in the calf. He reached in his holster and grabbed the .357 Magnum and fired off the remaining slugs in the direction of the muzzle flash. When his gun was empty he rolled toward the Jeep. He felt Jeff dragging him by his coat sleeve to safety behind the Jeep.

Jeff grabbed Avery and pulled him to the relative safety of the Jeep and said, "Where are you shot? Are you OK?"

Avery was hurting so bad he couldn't speak but was able to get out, mumbling, "The unknown person I was worried about!" He tried to get up, but the pain in his ribs jolted him back down. He knew he must have a couple of cracked, maybe even broken, ribs. Avery noticed he wasn't bleeding, and when he reached inside his parka he found the piece of metal from what was left of the boathouse propane tank. He had totally forgotten about it, and when he felt it he started laughing, never having believed it would save his life. The irony of the event struck him funny, and he started laughing, harder, but it hurt.

Jeff looked at Avery laughing and thought he must be cracking under pressure and said, "Keep down. Whoever this guy is, he's got us pinned down. We're in deep kaka, buddy." He raised up a little and peeked around the back of the Jeep to see if he could spot the shooter, and another shot rang out. He could feel the buzz of a bullet go by his ear. That was the second time that had happened tonight and he was starting to get pissed off. He aimed his .38 and fired off three quick shots in the direction of the shooter and got about four back in return. He scooted back behind the Jeep, and another three quick shots hit the Jeep. He heard a headlight get smashed out. One of the running lights exploded, and pieces of glass flew out behind them. A couple more shots hit the Jeep's back gate, making thudding sounds as they landed.

Avery had worked himself back to his feet and said, "Do you think you can get to that hill off to our right if I cover you? I would, but I don't think I could run to the other side of the Jeep right now in my condition."

Jeff looked toward the hill and back to where the shooter was and said, "If you can keep him busy for about ten seconds, I think I could get in a better position to see him." He got in a sprinter's position and said, "Let me know when you're ready."

Avery reloaded his gun and positioned himself at the back of the Jeep, keeping snugly close. He raised the gun and held it securely and said, "Go!"

As soon as Jeff started moving, Avery reached out to the side of the Jeep and started firing as fast as he could. The shooter returned fire very quickly, and Avery dove back behind the Jeep. He looked for Jeff but couldn't see him right away and finally spotted him creeping up the hill. Avery knew whoever was shooting at them was very good. He silently regretted making the decision to go after the sniper and thought about calling the plan off.

Jeff worked his way up the small hill and when he was near the top motioned Avery to get ready for another volley. They both reloaded and when Avery was ready he gave Jeff the signal. They both fired at the same time, and Avery could see small sparks bouncing off the bridge facing and railing. He thought for a minute that he saw someone standing on top of the bridge but had to duck for cover quickly. He regretted the plan again, thinking the sniper was also moving to a better position.

The shooter returned their fire quickly and kept firing. He fired at Avery and then at Jeff. They kept low, waiting for the chance to fire off another volley. Avery wondered if the sniper was changing positions, because it was suddenly very quiet. He was getting ready to signal Jeff to wait when they heard a loud bang come from the direction of the shooter. Avery thought, *Oh, shit, he got a bigger gun.*

They waited, but no more shots came and after a short while Avery stuck his gun out and blindly fired off two shots. There was silence again. Jeff raised up and looked to where the shooter was and quickly plopped back down. No shots were returned.

Avery whistled up to Jeff and, when he got his attention, held up his arms in a questioning posture, which sent searing stabs of pain down his side and into his ribs. Jeff shook his head negatively and started back down the hill. He worked his way near the Jeep and said, "What happened? Do you think we got him?"

Avery, gasping for breath, said, "I don't know. It sounded like his rifle exploded or he got a bigger gun." He looked around the Jeep and popped back, but no shots rang out.

Jeff scooted back to the rear of the Jeep and nothing happened. They decided to wait a little while and then got ready for a couple more shots, but it was quiet. Avery raised himself on his tiptoes and looked over the top of the Jeep, but he couldn't see anything. They both squatted down on their haunches and talked about what to do next.

They agreed to run in the direction of the shooter, taking cover along the way. They decided that they couldn't stay where they were because they didn't know whether the shooter was heading for them or they had gotten lucky with one of their shots. Either way, they had to find out.

Avery headed to the left and Jeff kept to the hill side of the road. They gradually worked their way to a spot where they could see the overpass cement base, but they couldn't see anyone. Jeff took the bold move of running up to the base of the concrete support. When he got there Avery was right behind him with his gun ready to fire. They couldn't see anyone. They worked their way under the expressway, where they could see spent cartridge shells all over the place, but no sniper. Jeff took out his cigarette lighter and shined it around, and they spotted a lot of blood on the ledge about five feet over their heads. Jeff followed the trail of blood on the ground to the other end of the cement base. The trail continued around the corner and up the hill to the expressway up above, and that's where the trail of blood ended. They both squatted and looked up when they heard a car pass overhead.

They headed back to the Jeep, and Jeff said, "Whoever it is won't last long, not with all the blood he's lost. Even if he had a car up on the expressway, he'll never make it to a hospital."

Avery kept his eyes open for any movement and when he was confident they were alone said, "Just as long as he's gone. He had us in a bad situation there, and I don't care if he makes it or not."

Jeff remained silent as they approached the bridge.

Avery put on his gloves and started tossing debris from the Lincoln's trunk over the railing. Jeff went over to the snowbank and retrieved a small leather suitcase about the size of a carry-on luggage bag. He opened it up and whistled to himself and reached inside.

Avery walked over to see what held Jeff's attention and smiled when he saw what was in the bag. It was full of $100, $50, $20, and $10 bills, all tightly bound with string and wrapped in plastic. It was all used money. Jeff figured there must be about $200,000 in the bag. Jeff looked at the money and then to Avery. He asked, "What should we do with it? Toss it?"

Avery started walking back to the Jeep and said, "You found it; you decide. I got what I wanted and it's over as far as I'm concerned."

Jeff started toward the railing and stopped. He was deep in thought and after a while headed to the Jeep. He tossed the bag in the back of the Jeep and was ready to get in when Avery said, "Quiet a minute."

He stood outside the Jeep craning his neck and after a while asked, "There, did you hear that?"

Jeff got out of the Jeep and walked up next to Avery and listened. They both stood there holding their breath and not moving, to see if they could hear anything. They both heard the sound at the same time.

The sound came from the ravine, and they walked to the railing and looked over.

"Help! Is anyone up there?"

The voice was weak and sounded far-off. Avery looked over to Jeff and said, "I don't believe someone survived that crash."

He looked over the railing again and could see the fire down below burning itself out.

The voice came again. "Someone help me. I'm stuck in the car and can't get out. My legs are broken and I think my arms are, too. If you help me, I'll make it worth your time."

Avery leaned over the railing and Jeff grabbed him by the coattail, holding him back. Avery yelled down to the voice, "Who are you? What's your name?"

They listened for a long time and were wondering if whoever it was had died when the voice said, "Carlyle, Manny Carlyle." There was a moment of silence, and Manny called out, "I've got over $200,000 and it's yours if you get me out of here and to a hospital!"

They could hear Manny coughing down below, and Avery cursed, saying, "Son of a bitch! That bastard won't die."

Jeff walked over to the Jeep with a determined expression on his face. When he came back he was smoking a cigarette and had the small wad of C-4 explosive Avery had put under the driver's side seat.

Avery looked at the C-4 and asked, "What are you going to do with that?"

Jeff smiled while smoking the cigarette and said, "I told you this stuff might come in handy." He looked at the cigarette and took a couple more drags on it and got the tip extremely hot. He took what was left of the cigarette and stuck the filter end into the C-4. He handed it to Avery and said, "You want justice? Here's your chance to get it."

Avery took the deadly bundle and walked to the bridge railing. He leaned over and dropped the C-4 package toward the spot where the Lincoln rested. They both looked over the railing and watched, but nothing happened. Avery thought it had missed and was about to tell Jeff so when he heard the muffled explosion that seemed to suck the air right out of his lungs.

Avery felt the air rush up into his face, causing him to blink rapidly while reeling back from the experience. He looked at Jeff and said, "Better down there on the Lincoln than under my Buick."

They both walked toward the Jeep as smoke from the C-4 explosion started rising up and over the railing. They looked around to make sure nobody was taking interest in what was going on and saw nothing. They got in the Jeep and headed out of the park, and Jeff laughed and said, "Better down there on the Lincoln than under the Buick. Why is that funny?"

Avery said nothing and started driving back to town. He remembered something and stopped the Jeep when they were under the expressway. He got out and reached in his parka and took out the gun Don had given him. He turned and fired the pistol until it was empty. Avery got back in the Jeep and continued driving. Jeff had watched what Avery did and when he got back in the Jeep asked him, "What was that all about?"

Avery was still having trouble breathing but responded, "It's an acknowledgment of a friend's favor."

Jeff accepted Avery's explanation at face value and said nothing.

50

To avoid any trouble Avery kept the Jeep at a reasonable speed while he drove back to town. It also helped keep down the wind coming through the missing windshield. They were both cold and Avery had the heater as high as it would go. The Jeep had suffered a lot of damage from the sniper, including a couple holes in the radiator, but it made it back to town, smoking and sputtering the last two miles or so.

When they got to the plaza the Buick was still there, but someone must have closed the door Jeff had left open when he tried to motion Crawley to follow him. It seemed perfectly fine. Jeff got out of the Jeep and went to the Buick. He stowed the bag of money in the trunk and started it up. He followed Avery to Don's service station, where Avery parked the Jeep well to the back of the station. He left a note on the front seat that read: "Don, I know it looks bad, but it had a rough night and did its part. Your little customizing job worked well also. Fix her up if you can. I'll call you. Thanks, Ave."

They went back to the plaza, and after making sure nobody was around, Avery got in Crawley's Mercedes-Benz and drove it out of town to a spot where someone was sure to find it during morning traffic.

Jeff drove to the medical clinic on the edge of town, where they got medical treatment after telling the clinic staff that they were injured in a snowmobile accident. The two drove home after being patched up. Avery was under heavy medication and felt no pain during the drive home.

By the time they got back to Avery's house it was 3:00 A.M. They both checked the house for any traps someone, anyone,

168

might have set while they were out.

Avery would spend the next two weeks sleeping in a sitting position because it was too painful to sleep lying down. Jeff spent the same amount of time walking with a limp.

51

Walt Beyer left the firehouse and was on his way to pick up some camping supplies he had ordered earlier that day from the local supermarket. As soon as the truck was loaded, he planned on heading out to the hunting camp for some winter rabbit hunting, as well as some serious drinking with some of his friends from the firehouse. He was ready to make a turn onto the county road when he spotted Avery Profrock's Jeep heading out of town at a high rate of speed. Walt watched the Jeep go by and wondered what Avery's big hurry was. Walt was ready to make the turn toward town when he spotted a big Lincoln Town Car coming up behind the Jeep and someone was shooting at it. Deciding to see what the hell was going on, he turned the steering wheel and headed out after the Lincoln.

Walt's pickup truck was old and had seen better days, but it was dependable. When he tried to catch up with the speeding cars he knew the old truck was no match for them. The truck could only get up to sixty miles an hour with the help of a stiff tailwind. He did his best and kept the Lincoln's taillights in view, but the Jeep was out of sight. Avery had a big engine in that thing and it could outrun almost anything, especially in winter conditions. Walt kept up the best he could, but when the Lincoln turned off the country road onto the expressway he momentarily lost it. He picked it up again when he followed the entrance ramp. The Lincoln was building up speed, and when it went around one of the many bends in the expressway Walt lost them again. He kept going, keeping a watchful eye for the Lincoln, but couldn't find it. He was considering turning around and heading back to town, but something told him that Avery was in trouble and he decided to keep going.

He was about three miles past the Gorge Park exit when he spotted what looked like the Lincoln, but when he got close he realized it was an old Pontiac. He wondered if they had gotten off one of the exit ramps and turned the truck around to backtrack. He was about halfway to the park exit when the right front tire went flat and he cursed for not having Don replace it last week when he had the truck inspected. Don had told him the tire was marginal and he should have it replaced. He pulled to the side of the road and was changing the tire when he heard what sounded like gunshots. He tried to hear where they were coming from, but the shots echoed all around the hilly terrain. There was no traffic on the expressway, and it seemed awfully quiet except for the echoes. Walt thought of Avery and hoped he wasn't in some kind of trouble, then finished changing the tire as fast as he could and jumped back in the truck. He headed in the direction he thought the shots were coming from.

When Walt got near the park he slowed down and rolled down the window. He could hear more shots being fired close by. He kept driving, trying to zero in on where the shots were coming from. He drove past the park entrance and realized he had gone too far. He turned the truck around and headed back to the park entrance and stopped. The shots were very close, and he pulled the truck to the shoulder of the road. He grabbed his shotgun from behind the seat and loaded both barrels. Walt opened the door quietly and got out of the truck. He didn't hear any shots and walked over to the railing to get a view of the road leading to the park entrance.

When he looked over the railing he immediately spotted Avery's Jeep parked on the park entrance road just past the gorge bridge. Its running lights were on, and he could see that the Jeep had been shot up. Walt looked everywhere but couldn't see the Lincoln and wondered where it was. Walt noticed that the Jeep was running and the exhaust left a billowing cloud in the cold night air. He was looking around trying to see where Avery might be when shots were fired from behind the Jeep. One of the shots hit the railing near Walt's position on the overpass, and he jumped back and squatted.

He was about to get up again to get a better view when he heard several shots coming from underneath the overpass directly below where he was standing. He looked over to where the Jeep was and recognized Avery's parka and someone else was with him. He didn't know what was going on but understood that Avery and whoever was with him were in serious trouble. They were pinned down by whoever was under the overpass, and it sounded like the shooter down there had a high-powered rifle. Given time, whoever it was would kill Avery and his friend.

Walt did some quick thinking and ruled out getting a shot off at the sniper from the overpass railing because he might be spotted. He was also in Avery's line of fire. He decided to approach the sniper from behind, and after checking to see if any cars were in the area, he ran across the parkway to the other side of the overpass.

Walt carefully descended the small hill and hid behind the cement support brace when he got to ground level. He heard more shots while peeking around and spotted the sniper. The guy was lying on the top of the cement brace directly under the huge steel support beams and had a rifle with what looked like a night scope. He was taking aim and Walt knew that Avery and his friend were going to be dead soon if he didn't take this guy out.

Walt looked around again for the Lincoln, but it wasn't here either. He silently wondered how this guy got here and wouldn't figure it out until the next spring, when the Lincoln was discovered at the bottom of the gorge.

Walt was glad there was no snow under the bridge because it would have made tough footing as he was sneaking up on the guy. He worked his way along the cement brace, and when he was directly below the sniper he raised the shotgun carefully and fired at point-blank range.

The sniper never knew what hit him. The impact from the blast lifted the sniper about two feet off his vantage point. When he came down he tumbled to the base of the support, his rifle tumbling down after him.

Walt looked over to the Jeep and wondered what to do. He

decided to get out of there in case the police showed up and took exception to his action. He decided to take the sniper with him.

Walt grabbed the sniper and the rifle and headed back to the truck. When he got to the top of the hill and was near the railing he heard a car approach. He froze in his tracks, thinking the Lincoln had returned, but when he looked he spotted a police cruiser slowly passing by. He squatted down to avoid being detected. He hoped Avery and his friend didn't fire off any shots or they all would be in deep trouble, but it was silent and the cruiser passed by without taking interest. Walt's racing heart slowed down and he could breathe again.

Walt scooted over the railing and quickly deposited the dead guy in the back of the truck. He wrapped the body in an old painting tarp and closed the gate. He was glad to have the cap on the truck so nobody could see inside. He grabbed the dead man's rifle and threw it behind the seat along with his shotgun and got out of there as fast as he could. He took one last look in the rearview mirror but still didn't see the Lincoln anywhere.

Walt went back to town like nothing had happened and picked up the camping supplies. He decided to dispose of the body when he got to the hunting camp. There was a spot near the edge of camp where he could get rid of the body without it ever being found.

Walt drove to the cabin and was glad to see that Mr. Gorban had plowed the road out. Walt had called him yesterday and asked him to plow it out, telling him that he and some friends were coming up for some hunting and drinking. He told the old man to stop by if he had a chance, but he declined.

Walt looked all around the site and, when he was sure he was alone, took the tarp-wrapped body out of the back of the truck and headed to the dumping spot. The dump was actually a deep crevice in the huge rocks on the edge of camp where things disappeared, never to return. The dump was a long walk, but Walt hardly worked up a sweat.

When he got to the site he took out the flashlight he got from the truck glove box and shined it in the dead man's face and recognized him. He couldn't remember where he had seen him before. Walt reached down and got out the dead man's wallet and opened it. When he opened the wallet he was suddenly reminded of a Harrison Ford movie where a little kid in a baseball cap was looking up and saying, "Uh-oh! Indy, big trouble," because Walt was looking at the dead man's FBI identification card.

Walt stood there for a moment wondering if he had made a big mistake sticking his nose in Avery's business. He searched the wallet and found $1,200 and wondered what this guy was doing with so much money. He shined the flashlight back in the guy's face and said, "What have you been up to, Mr. FBI man? Why were you trying to kill my friend?"

Walt took another look at the guy and suddenly remembered that this was one of the feds that had given Captain Highgate an ulcer the day after Karen and her niece were killed in the explosion and fire. He wasn't the guy in charge, but Walt remembered that this guy found a lot of things to laugh about while everyone else was sick to their stomach and feeling totally miserable. After a while Walt figured that this guy must have had something to do with the deaths of Karen and her niece and Avery had found out about it. This was all the justification Walt needed, and he picked up the body and lowered it into the narrow crevice and dropped it. He waited until he heard the sound of the body hitting the bottom of the crevice, then picked up the tarp and headed back to the cabin. He stopped on the way and tossed the tarp in a large metal barrel used to burn trash and set it on fire. Then he took the dead man's wallet and removed the money. He tossed it in with the tarp and waited until it was reduced to ashes. Before leaving, he looked down and spotted an envelope on the ground and picked it up. The envelope contained $10,000 in $100 bills. It must have fallen out of the tarp, and Walt wondered who had paid the guy to kill Avery. On his way back to the cabin he thought about Avery and his friend out at the Gorge Park, hoping they got the guy who paid the sniper.

After Walt had all the camping supplies stored away, he sat in front of the fireplace drinking a beer and decided he'd buy a new fishing boat with his financial windfall. After all, the dead man wouldn't have any need for the money.

52

Jason and Spike couldn't believe their luck. They had spent the whole day cruising the parking lots and plazas looking for one good car to snatch, but everywhere they went someone was keeping an eye on them. Spike laughed and said, "Our reputation precedes us. It's nice to be recognized, but not this much."

Jason decided to head out of town and back to the trailer park. He looked at Spike and said, "Hey, man, tomorrow's another day. We'll find something that will get us enough money to make that coke score. And when we do, we'll be rolling in dough."

They were a little high and playing the radio as loud as it could be turned up when Spike said, "Look, man. Do you see what I see?"

Jason looked over at the intersection and saw the Mercedes-Benz sedan and pulled over to the side of the road. He looked around and said to Spike, "Not a soul around and that beauty is ripe for picking."

They both looked around again and couldn't see another car anywhere. They got out of the Camaro and walked over to the Mercedes and looked inside.

Jason whistled and said, "Bad news, man. There's a guy in there with a hole in his head."

Spike looked in and laughed. He said, "Good, man, saves us the trouble. This beauty will bring us over ten grand at the chop shop in Jamestown, and look; the keys are in the ignition. What are we waiting for?"

Jason said, "Fuckin'-a-right, man." He opened the Mercedes door and pushed Crawley's body over and started it up. He told Spike, "You take the Camaro and follow me. When we get to the

Gorge River Bridge we'll toss this dude over and head for Jamestown."

Before they tossed Crawley's body over the bridge they removed his wallet, with over a thousand dollars in it, and got his service revolver as a bonus.

Six months later Jason and Spike would disappear after crossing the wrong people in a drug deal.

Crawley's body would never be found.

Spring

Jeff and Winnie were moved into the new house on Merrygold Lane. The workman were busy building the antique shop, which was being attached to the front of the boathouse.

Winnie had busied herself the last few months selling the old house and getting things ready to be moved. She was delighted to be here at the lake in spring and looked forward to the challenge of starting a new business. Avery was their partner, but they didn't see much of him since he had started his new book.

Heather was helping Winnie move in and shopping for all the things she and Jeff would need for the shop. They had become good friends, and Winnie liked having Heather and Avery as neighbors.

One afternoon while Winnie and Heather were eating lunch outside in the fresh spring air, Winnie asked Heather, "Have you told Avery yet?"

Heather smiled and said with excitement in her voice, "Yes, and he's been acting like a silly goose ever since I told him."

Winnie laughed a little and, smiling, said, "Yes, I bet. Most men act that way when they find out they're about to become a father." She hesitated a little and after some thought asked Heather, "Has Avery ever told you what happened that night last winter when he broke those two ribs?"

Heather thought for a minute, then answered, "No. And I don't think I really want to know. I think it had something to do with Karen's death though. Asking might make him remember, and I don't want that."

Winnie reached over and touched Heather's hand and said,

"Good. Some things are better left alone. He'll tell you about it someday when he's ready."

She remembered the story that Jeff had told her shortly after he returned from the lake last winter and knew it was better if she helped him put it behind them, so she did.

A week or so after the incident at the Gorge Park, Jeff counted the money in the leather bag. It contained $360,000. He made arrangements to have the money deposited in Avery's bank and made out three cashier's checks for $120,000 each. He mailed them to the families of the three agency men killed at Goldylock's House.

About two weeks after Jeff returned home, he and Winnie were making arrangements to sell the house and move to the lake. One day a representative of the federal prosecutor's office visited Jeff and informed him that Franklin Crawley had disappeared. The man offered Jeff his job back with full benefits and the possibility of replacing Crawley.

Jeff declined the offer and instead put in for all vacation and personal time and applied for his pension. It was accepted by the agency, and Jeff would be eligible for fourteen months of full pay before retirement benefits began.

Shortly after Jeff and Winnie moved to the lake, Jeff was visited by Bill Trusk from the Buffalo office of the FBI. Trusk asked if Jeff had any knowledge as to the whereabouts of Franklin Crawley since his disappearance about five months ago.

Jeff was considering telling Trusk that he might look for Manny Carlyle, because he had heard that the two were in business together. He thought about telling Trusk that Manny and Crawley had been making a lot of trips to South America together but, instead, replied, "No, I haven't seen Mr. Crawley since we met last fall and he relieved me of duty."

Trusk then asked him if he knew the whereabouts of an agent, Bob Stern, who had disappeared about the same time as Mr. Crawley.

Jeff said he never knew Agent Stern, but if he heard anything he would contact the Buffalo office and let Trusk know.

Jeff told Trusk, "I don't know if you're aware or not, but I no longer work with the Witness Protection Program and am officially retired."

Trusk said, "Yes, I am aware of your retirement. I am also aware that you got a raw deal from Crawley, and whatever happened to him . . . " He stopped talking and looked around to see if anyone was listening, then continued, "This is off the record of course. He deserved it." Trusk started leaving and before he got in his agency car asked, "By the way, you wouldn't know where Manny Carlyle is, would you? He seems to have disappeared, too."

Jeff smiled at Trusk and said, "You know something, Trusk? You ask too many questions."

Trusk got in his car and rolled down the window and said, "Maybe you're right; then again, maybe I'm asking the wrong person." He waited for Jeff to say something and when he got no reply started the engine and said, "As far as I'm concerned, this case revolves around Manny Carlyle, and if he ever shows up, I'll have a talk with him. If he can't tell me anything, well, then I guess I'll have to close this case."

Jeff nodded at Trusk in understanding as he watched him drive off.

When Trusk was gone Jeff thought about what had happened the last six or seven months and how things had turned out. He reflected on the results and finally concluded that doing things Avery's way, radical as they were, got the job done.

Walt Beyer had watched Jeff as he talked with the FBI agent. Walt recognized Trusk as being the agent in charge the day he and Captain Highgate were ordered off the fire investigation. Walt didn't know what they were talking about and continued waxing his new boat while glancing over once in a while. He got the distinct impression that Jeff was not being totally cooperative with Trusk and that suited him just fine, because he had resolved to never tell Avery or anyone else about the night at the gorge. It was over, and the sooner forgotten, the better.

A few weeks later Manny's Lincoln was discovered at the

bottom of the gorge ravine. Walt would be assigned to the safety crew when rescue workers brought in a big crane to hoist the car out. Any doubts or reservations Walt had about the night at the gorge park were erased when he learned about Manny and his business dealings.

Manny's Lincoln had been discovered by some hikers late in April after the spring floodwaters receded. The three bodies found in the car were burned beyond recognition. Damage caused by floodwaters and decomposition made identification of the bodies difficult. Autopsies and examination of dental records eventually identified the bodies as those of Manny and his two men who were reported missing months earlier. The medical examiner's report ruled the cause of death as accidental as the result of multiple injuries from the accident and resulting fire.

Local police authorities who investigated the incident stated that the driver of the Lincoln must have lost control on the icy roads sometime during the winter months. The Lincoln apparently went off the Chautauqua Gorge State Park entrance road and crashed into the ravine. The official accident report stated that foul play had been ruled out in the incident and no further investigation was warranted.

Avery was busy working on his new book about the fictional drug trafficker who got involved with a corrupt government official and how they both paid the supreme price for crossing a professional killer. He was being careful about how he wrote the book and found it hard to concentrate since Heather told him she was pregnant.

He had been having a bout of depression about his new relationship with Heather and decided to have her move in with him after he visited Karen's gravesite. During the visit he sensed her presence and knew that she would have approved of his new life and the depression faded.

Avery had a new purpose in life now and knew he must go forward. Karen would never be forgotten and would forever hold a special place in his memories.

When the baby was born in late summer, Heather surprised

him by naming her Karen Desiree and he knew all was good in the world again.

Don returned Avery's Jeep about six weeks after the night at the gorge. He told Avery the story behind the old gun and they both agreed to write a book about it. However, Don was found dead in his office later that year and Avery would be launched into another adventure while investigating the circumstances.

NEXT BOOK

Randy sat in the kitchen of his mother's apartment in Erie, Pennsylvania, enjoying the fine spring day and reading the account of Manny Carlyle's death. He finished the newspaper article and sat smiling to himself remembering the conversation he had with the stranger on the pay phone outside Pete's Hoagie House last fall. He picked up the paper again and reread the part where foul play had been ruled out and smiled broadly. He clapped his hands and laughed a little.

Randy's mother came into the kitchen and said, "Lord, child, what has come over you? You look like the cat that caught the canary. I haven't seen you smile like that in a long, long time. What is it?"

Randy got up from the chair and walked over to his mom and gave her a big hug and said, "You know, Mom, there are some good guys left in the world."

His mom smiled at her son even though she had no idea what he was talking about. It didn't matter, because she was glad to see him happy again, and a tear fell from her eye.

Randy was getting ready to go to work and before leaving said, "Mom, I'm taking you out to dinner tonight. You got a date with your favorite man."

As Randy left the apartment, he heard his mother humming to herself in the kitchen. It was a familiar sound that he hadn't heard since his older brother was accidentally killed in a drug-related shooting almost two years ago. He walked to work thinking about his big brother and how much he still missed him. He also thought about the stranger on the phone and silently thanked him.